Stoneheart

ALSO BY C.M. BANSCHBACH

The Dragon Keep Chronicles
Oath of the Outcast
Blood of the Seer

The Drifter Duology
Then Comes A Drifter
A Name Long Buried

Spirits' Valley Duology
Greywolf's Heart
Saber's Pride

Drax Guard: Crew Six
Flashpoint
Faultline
Conduit

STONE HEART

DRAX GUARD: CREW SIX #4

C.M. BANSCHBACH

Stoneheart

Copyright © 2025 by C.M. Banschbach

All rights reserved.

ISBN: 979-8-9890651-4-1

Published by Campitor Press

clairembanschbach.com

Cover Design: Emilie Haney @eahcreative

Drax Guard Logo: Morlin Lorenz @thatmoonysky

For Jenni.

1

Dejan

Whoever says hearts are simple can jump off a cliff. I stare at my phone screen and the message that has been there for at least ten minutes. I've got knees pulled up, arm flung over them, hiding it from Remy who sits next to me on the train car floor.

Sergeant Cieran O'Donnell sleeps opposite me, slouched against his pack, ballcap on backwards over dark hair slightly longer than standard military cut. His arms are crossed over his chest, and his hand rests on the knife strapped to the front of his armored tac vest.

Communications Specialist Besim Antilles is somewhere up front, chatting with part of the train crew. The towering half-troll on our squad makes friends everywhere he goes. Thankfully it's gotten him away from me, taking the mournfully observant looks with him.

Specialist Remy Kalama sprawls against his pack, fingers drumming against his thigh as he skims through some messages on his phone. At least he's sitting next to me and not constantly spooked to see me existing.

I should be more irritated by their behavior. But in the three months since I got hit in the heart by a high-powered spell from Remy's crazy fae ex after she kidnapped their kid, I've been progressively losing all emotion and feeling.

No one knows how bad it is. I sort of have the reputation for being stoic and grumpy anyway. Some people think it's an elf thing, but maybe I am just bitter and warped inside. Elves normally live to about two hundred years old, and most of my forty-five haven't had many positive highlights.

Sometimes *I* don't even realize how bad it is. I've never really been one for strong displays of emotion anyway. But this is something different.

My gaze falls back to the phone, screen black since I'd forgotten about it in the last two minutes. The message reappears when I unlock the phone.

-I heard about what happened. Just checking in.-

This is the second message I've gotten from my old crew sergeant Pothos Allaire in the last week. It's him checking in and not a family member. Because my dad's in federal prison and my cousin would be throwing a party to celebrate me dying if he wasn't the one finishing me off himself. One other person might care, but I haven't seen her in years. She might be co-hosting the party for all I know. And I wouldn't blame her.

I turn the phone over, hiding the message. If Pothos heard about my injury, that means someone's been talking. It probably wasn't Cieran. He doesn't know me well enough yet. He's only been our squad sergeant for nine months. Hell, Rem and Bes really only know me from the last five years of being on the same spec ops Drax Guard crew together. They barely know anything about me from before we were teammates, except that I spent a few years as Army medic, and before that as a paramedic in Dunhare and nearby Portland. Nothing about the majority of my life in Detroit.

And they definitely don't know how bad I've gotten yet. Don't know that I'm slowly getting locked further inside my own mind. That I've been struggling to perform basic functions and tasks every day for the last three months. Made more difficult in the two weeks we've been prepping to go on mission with the knowledge that as team medic, it's on me to take care of them if something happens. I'm already halfway crippled, but I can't just give up yet. Won't just walk away like I have before. Not until I'm physically unable to.

It's probably Captain Bron Wolfe, the Drax Guard commander, who snitched on me. He's got access to my personnel file—sealed at a higher level than most of the rest of the Guard—and Pothos is listed as my emergency contact. Something a little simpler now that we aren't running missions together.

Like I said, my family and I don't have a lot of love for each other. Not after I made sure to wreck their plans and drug empire and offer one last middle finger on my way out of Detroit. Pothos is the one who'll have to manage all my stuff after I'm gone, make sure it gets to the right people.

Maybe I should reply.

Motion draws my attention to Cieran. He flinches in his sleep. Remy looks up, instantly alert. Cieran's hands twitch, then one closes tight around the knife, and he jolts awake. Sucks in a breath and pushes more upright.

The bigger part of me idly wonders what happened, why he looks so spooked. And it's like the smallest part of me beats against the rising brick wall in the back of my mind, telling me to ask if he's okay, distract him with some sarcastic comment. But that voice is slowly getting drowned out by the increasingly louder white noise in my head.

Remy beats me to it. "Okay, Sarge?"

Cieran knocks his hat off, scrubbing at his eyes and raking a hand through his dark hair before jamming it on backwards again.

"Yeah." But he doesn't sound convinced. He spins the copper-inlaid bracelet around his wrist. Heartbond dampener.

We've been tracking down the remnants of a child trafficking ring for the last three months after taking down a fae named Maeve Ballagh. The same one who left me with this...condition. The info we got from that mission linked some smugglers to the Kirnae dragonwalker islands, resulting in a team-up with one of their fleets.

A member of which Cieran is heartbonded to. They're sort of disgustingly perfect for each other. The back of my mind refuses to flinch at the reminder of heartbonds. It had been a punch in the gut to see theirs activate when we met the dragonwalker fleet in the Allied States Wastelands eleven months ago. Athina had been the thing to help pull Cieran out of a mental pit a mile deep after losing his old crew to a terrorist, and then his sister to cancer.

But they have to wear bond dampeners when on missions for security reasons. Different countries, different spec ops forces. They'd never use the information against each other, but higher-ups don't know or don't care about that. We're headed to meet up with Athina's crew now, and a team from the Bureau of Magical Affairs will join later once we make it to the predetermined coordinates along the A.S.-Mexican border.

Once their boots are on the ground, the dampener is coming off and we have to deal with the two of them together.

"Where's Bes?" Cieran asks, still trying to shake off the nightmare. He rubs his right knee where his prosthetic lower leg is spliced to nerve endings and skin for a permanent limb replacement.

Remy inclines his head up front. "Probably giving a group therapy session to the crew."

A grin swerves across Cieran's face. We've all been on the receiving end of Besim's quiet questions and support. You'd think a six-foot-five, longsword-carrying, half-troll would be all about fighting and winning. Trolls have always been notoriously competitive. But the guy barely curses and uses violence as a last resort. If anyone was smart, they'd make him a negotiator. He'd have peace on earth in a week and we'd all be out of a job.

Cieran checks his watch. We're almost there. If I had any sense, or cared at all, I'd have also been sleeping. Less time to try to pretend that I'm still myself. Remy still fiddles with his phone. Cieran glances at him and the corner of his mouth twitches.

"You ask her out yet?"

Remy's head flies up and his brown skin turns even darker. He's at least smart enough not to deny he knows what Cieran's talking about.

"No." There's definitely something like a squeak in his voice.

Say something. Something sarcastic. The faint *me* tries to break through again. The bit left that cares and wants to keep up the front that I'm the same as I always was.

But I have nothing. Besim saves me. He steps back into our small space through the sliding door. All trolls look human, with dark grey skin tougher than granite and towering over anything—especially shorter elves—at a minimum of six feet. We barely max out at five-ten. Besim's half-human side shows as tanned skin and dark hair, but his troll heritage gives him the stoneskin when in danger. It's tougher than our mail and armored tac vests, but he still wears the standard-issue armor.

He takes one look at Remy and guesses. "He hasn't asked her yet?"

Cieran laughs, head tossed back and gleeful. Remy throws a hand in the air, spitting out a few harmless stinging sparks from his fingertips and a light curse at Besim. The half-troll dodges the sparks and the curse easily and comes to crouch beside Cieran. Burn scarring from that same Wastelands mission traces down the left side of his jaw and neck. Wild magic ate *through* his stoneskin to burn him, and it really worried me and Rem when Besim had trouble after that mission.

I've finally got something.

"Give him a break, guys," I say.

Remy flings a hand at me in a pointed "thank you" motion.

"He still lives with his parents. How's he know how to ask a girl out?"

I get shoved over, but Remy shakes his head and grins through the laughter. My mouth moves.

Smiling. I'm smiling. Normal.

"Bear still obsessed with her?" Cieran asks. Underneath all the roasting, we're all incredibly protective of Remy and his four-year-old son. Especially after Blair got kidnapped and used as leverage against Remy three months ago. In five ears, I'd never seen Remy willingly talk to a woman outside of social niceties, and that made a lot of sense after meeting his ex.

But then along came Agent Sara Alder, the half-elf data analyst who helped with the Ballagh mission, threw herself right into harm's way to take care of Blair, and definitely made an impression on Remy.

He's been moving so slow he might as well be standing still. Saying they're friends. They definitely are, but they're both also denying the something else underneath. He says it's because of Blair. But we all know the real reason and would be running an intervention if he'd just jumped headlong into a relationship with Sara.

But that doesn't mean we can't tease him about how long it's actually taking him to initiate.

"Yeah." Remy flips his phone around and shows a picture. Sara holds the camera, angling it down at Bear and her sitting at a low table, the surface covered in bright drawings, markers, and colored pencils. There's also a plate of cookies. Blair grins, the same wide smile and dark eyes as his dad. But circles under his eyes mean the kid hasn't been sleeping well again, working through the trauma of three months ago. Probably the reason the agent is over again.

Cieran shakes his head. "How have you not asked her out, Rem?"

Remy squirms a little and tucks the phone away. He's probably going to give some bullshit answer about being focused for the last two weeks on leaving for this mission. But he doesn't.

"I just don't want to mess up. Can't do that to Bear."

"Or yourself?" Besim says quietly.

"Yeah. That. Why am I not just paying you for my therapy?" Remy says the last part lightly. Besim gives a small smile, blocky features easing with the expression.

Remy's fingers fidget together and we wait him out. "It's just...I've got Bear, and that's a big ask, right?" He glances around before quickly turning his attention back to his hands.

"She already likes him," Cieran says.

"Yeah. But is going from friends to something else harder with a kid already in the mix?" Remy's mouth tucks down. He's really worried about the possibility of Sara walking away if he takes a step forward. It's like he doesn't see the way she looks at him.

"You're overthinking it," Besim says bluntly.

Cieran twitches a smile and Remy shakes his head, but doesn't argue. Wheels squeak and we all tilt slightly sideways as the train starts to pull to a halt. Cieran and I adjust our ballcaps, both backwards, though it takes some conscious effort to not put mine on forward. Guess weird heart-calcifying magic makes you want to do things correctly.

Remy re-straps his tac vest over his dark grey fatigues. He always wears short sleeves over the light-weight chain mail shirt, and buffs the mail to darken it. His innate fire magic keeps him warm and adding too many layers turns him into a grouch. And if he's cold, we're screwed. Besim and I wear long-sleeved fatigues over our mail, his forearm bracers and my archer's brace keeping them in place. Cieran has a lightweight hooded shirt over his to hide the shine since it's still too warm for his usual hooded sweatshirt.

No matter how much we complain about the mail, wizard developers just turn up their elite noses and say that ancient warriors liked it. Like they'd know. We've all got sunglasses and neck scarves. Back home in Dunhare, autumn is bringing crisp chill and rain, but the rocky, sandy deserts just south of the Wastelands and at the border between the Allied States and Mexico haven't got the memo yet.

With a final squeal, the train halts. We stand, slinging packs over our shoulders, checking weapons. My broadsword taps my left leg in reassurance. I'll wait to string my carbon-fiber bow until we're out of here. A lock disengages and Besim and Cieran haul back the door. We jump down, boots stirring up dust among scrub brush and some loose shale that's trickled down from the nearby foothills.

Doors shut and with a mighty straining huff, the train stirs back, the triple crystals in the front locomotive sending out some steam as the warlock mechanics dump their water magic on it. It's an older style, but out here it's the thing that'll resist the corroding wear of dust and heat the most.

Cieran slides his sunglasses on. "Ready?"

The others nod and it takes a few seconds, and them staring at me, before I realize that I'm just standing there with bow in hands. I jolt and string it, trying to shake off the way their stares bore into me, trying to assess and evaluate. See what's wrong.

I definitely don't look at Remy, not ready to see the haunted look that's sure to have sprung back into his eyes. He's been stupidly blaming himself for months.

Cieran turns east, setting the pace. We fall into a loose diamond formation. I'm at the three o'clock, bow in hand. Fates, this place is boring. Even more boring than the Wastelands, a ragged scar slashing across the country divided by civil war before reuniting against newly wakened fire drakes. Those thousands of miles of ashy devastation still smoking from the war and a supervolcanic eruption two hundred years ago have eerie remnants of civilization and things to fight. This is desert and heat and *flat* as we leave the foothills of the mountains lurking behind us.

"Dej!"

I jolt, dragging my gaze up from the ground passing under my boots, and find them all looking back at me.

I've missed something. Something important?

I'm not sure who said my name. And they're not offering anything back. My feet scuff the dust, stirring it up almost as bad as the churning mess that's trying to force its way out. I'm not sure what it means, and I kind of hate it.

"What?" I finally say. Snap. Try to give some sort of emotion other than the monotone I've been noticing myself fall into recently.

Cieran taps the sunglasses up his nose, and hooks both hands in the collar of his vest. "What's going on with you, Dej?"

There's a tilt to his head, an edge to his voice that means he's checking in as a sergeant. Remy's already looking down, arms crossed and hands pressed flat against his sides—his reaction to not feeling in control. Besim's arms also cross, that same stoic expression on his face that can shift to caring or concerned in a split second.

"What do you mean?" I counter. The white noise fades and a bit of me comes back, ready to scuffle.

His feet brace a little wider. "I mean, you've missed the opportunity for three savage comebacks in the last twenty minutes—"

It's been twenty minutes?

"And the hell you holding your bow like that for?"

My attention turns down. The bow is loosely held in a careless grip in my left hand. I never put it back in its holster alongside my quiver, ready to be pulled out at a moment's notice. I pack it away, shrugging my shoulders.

"Just thinking."

"About?" The arch of Cieran's brow over his glasses is unyielding.

Remy barely looks at me. *Something* breaks through and I *feel* for a second.

"None of your Fates-crossed business." I whirl on Remy, and he jerks back in surprise. "And stop *firren* looking like that. You're not responsible for three months ago."

He regards me like I'm some strange thing.

I shake my head. "I'm fine. Still just a *shilsa*."

Cieran's mouth quirks. He knows the elvish curse. And he's not disagreeing with me. I'm that and worse, but they'll never know because

I'll never turn my back on them. Never vanish without a trace like I did to the only other person I ever cared about.

"We moving or not?" I ask.

"Let's go." Cieran spins on his heel and starts off again. Remy still gives me space, and Besim...he doesn't say anything. I want to snap at him to quit analyzing me, but then he'll ask some pointed question to make me think I need to be analyzed. But I'm already sinking back into the numbing hum.

At the next small rise spotted with trees, Cieran stops and takes his small pocket map and compass out, scanning the horizons and checking his markers.

"Okay." He folds it away. "Just waiting on the fleet."

2

Dejan

There's not much in the way of cover, a few growths that barely count as trees, but we make our way over. Cieran crouches, hands tucking back in his tac vest collar. Besim leans one shoulder against the tree trunk, and it manages to brace his weight. He takes a tablet from the front pocket of his vest to send the update back to our CO at the Dunhare Army base in Oregon. Remy faces the opposite direction, eyes out.

I step down the slight incline, still within sight line next to a tree with wispy leaves, and some thorny growths. It grows sideways, like the wind might have shoved it over in a fit of rage.

The way to avoid people seeing what's going on with me?

Avoid people.

Still nothing to see out here. We discovered that the trafficking ring has been using a route along the southern border, skirting the Wastelands, and heading over to the eastern half of the Allied States through Texas to drop their stolen kids for who knows what. They sent out a shipment two days ago, bringing us out here to intercept.

There are at least two dragonwalker kids in the group they're transporting, and these traffickers are going to get a nasty surprise when the Kirnae fleet drops in.

A faint scuff draws my attention to my left. Remy's there, arms crossed tight over his broad chest. I look away, back out into the vast emptiness. If there was anything out here at one time, it probably got wiped out or driven out during the fire drake war. This area would have been at the tail end of the violent fallout of magic and ash.

And I can see why no one's wanted to come back in the last two hundred years.

A huff draws my attention back to Remy. He's been watching me. His brown skin absorbs the sunlight, soaking it up to help fuel the wild magic coursing in his veins. His three-quarters Pacifica Islander heritage gives him an inherent mastery over fire magic, the swirling magma dragon tattoo on his left arm a testament to his people and their innate skills with fire and wild magic. The proximity to volcanic magma dragons now sleeping deep in the Earth's core gave the Hawaiian people magic decades ago, and has helped protect their kingdom from invasions over the centuries.

"What?" I finally ask, tired of overusing that word already.

He angles, standing shoulder to shoulder with me, a gulf of space between us like we haven't been as good as brothers for the last five years, serving in the same crew after surviving our Drax Guard Hell Week.

Well. Maybe that's rich coming from me, someone who left one or two good people behind before.

"Sure you're okay?" he asks, voice muted.

"Hell, Rem, how many times do I have to say it?"

"Until we all believe it."

Heat picks up around me and he's probably trying to see right into this thick head of mine. I don't talk to a lot of people outside the crew for various reasons. Rem's been the buffer between me and the world for the last four years. I trust him—and Bes—more than I've ever trusted anyone. And that's why I can't bring myself to admit to this yet. It feels like letting them down.

"Consider this that time."

Some sort of grunt comes from him, but he doesn't press. At least he knows not to keep bothering me.

"Don't think I will."

Well. Maybe not.

A low whistle comes from Cieran, and we join him and Besim. He slides the bond dampener off his wrist and sucks in a deep inhale, a faint smile playing over his face. Remy and Besim exchange a look. Three months ago, I'd be in on it too, about to start giving our sergeant absolute crap for being so damn smitten with his heartbonded warrior.

But I just stand there, barely raising a hand to block the dust as an aerial shape plunges into a descent, plummeting until even the others with human vision can see her red dragon scales. She shifts from dragon form a few feet above the ground and lands. Athina Spera, dragonwalker scout, hell of a good fighter, and just as smitten with Cieran.

"Show-off." He grins.

She brushes a bit of dust off her armor, an old-school breastplate with modern harness, coated in a dull sheen that reduces visibility. Bracers are strapped over her sleeves, the same tan color as the trousers, and sturdy calf-high boots. Three similarly attired dragonwalkers land behind her. Black, green, and shimmering white scales fade away to reveal the same crew we fought alongside almost a year ago in the Wastelands. Their dark skin has a coppery tone, matched in their sharp eyes that glint in direct light, betraying their shifter nature.

Her fleet captain, Dimos Kostas, nods to the rest of us. He's by the book—even his uniform looks straight-laced—so Remy and Besim get a "Specialist," and I get a "Corporal."

Iosef Buros heads over to Besim, both looming over the rest of us. In a surprise to absolutely no one, the two of them bonded over being the even-keeled mothers of the group. He's also got a heartbond dampener around his wrist to protect his wife while he's on missions, and a bit of additional magic to supplement the shifter power.

Restless energy always surrounds Takis Lagana, and the guy constantly fidgets with anything. Especially the extra knives he's got strapped on, like his dragon form isn't enough to take care of a threat. He slaps Remy's hand, sliding into a handshake. It takes a second for me to return the same greeting to him. And he tilts his head, the action somewhere between cat-like and a snake reading weakness in prey.

Cieran and Athina are next to each other, leaning close, eyes bright. Her dampener is off as well, but they're not quite filling the slight space between them. The same coppery color threads her dark hair wrapped in a braid around the crown of her head.

"Just get it over with." Takis sighs. Athina glares at her fleetmate, but Cieran grins like an idiot. He pulls her in for a kiss that she wholeheartedly returns to a chorus of groans and gags from the others. He lifts one hand up to flash a sign that she mimics, lifting one hand from around his shoulders to make sure we all see it.

That same slight pang still sneaks through whenever I see them together. Heartbonded, perfectly in tune with each other, knowing the other's thoughts almost before they do. Strength to weakness, like to like. They pull apart, foreheads pressing for a moment, and I turn away, not really having to stuff the jealousy and sadness down because it's already fading.

"How was the flight?" Besim asks. The dragonwalkers roll out their shoulders, and check weapons. Somehow they can shift in and out of their fifty-foot dragon forms and keep weapons, packs, and clothes with them.

"Uneventful." Dimos cracks his neck. Their archipelago sits off the coasts of Africa and Lusitania, and they got advance permission to portal gate from the Islands over to one of our Texas bases and fly the rest of the way.

The dragonwalkers pull out their own scarves, but apparently they don't believe in hats or sunglasses. They've brought comms, and Besim gives them our frequency. The fleet uses telepathy to communicate with each other, but that's no good for the rest of us. Cieran dodges Athina's attempts to turn his ballcap the right way forward. He gets far enough away and Athina grudgingly makes way for her fleet captain to start discussing logistics.

Athina joins in the muted conversations between our crews. Some glances are thrown at me, but I don't really feel like faking interest in the catch-up game, bringing everyone up to speed on families, leave time, and anything else in-between. Even off-duty, my life still completely revolves around the crew.

Suddenly those glances are a little more pointed at me. I narrow my eyes behind the glasses, still not joining in, but letting my sharper elf hearing tune in. Listening. They'd arrived for a planned joint training shortly after the mission to get Blair and Agent Alder back. I hadn't been released back to active duty yet by the time the exercises were done, and they went home with the info that led us to this moment. They must not have heard all the details about the curse, but they're hearing the rest now.

"I thought something smelled different about him." Takis.

"Cieran's right. That does sound weird." Remy's faint laugh doesn't quite hide his guilt.

"What do the doctors know?" Athina asks. She'd stayed on for a short visit and Cieran doesn't keep much of anything from her.

"Still not much." Besim's murmur is closer to a grumble, still painfully audible.

"So what's wrong with him?" Iosef, about to go full mama dragon if his posture and voice is any clue.

"He insists he's fine." A creak of chain mail against armored vest announces Besim's shrug. The heat is already wicking away some of the oil for the mail to keep it weatherproofed.

"Hmm." A humming growl breaks from one of the dragonwalkers.

Three months ago, I'd be cussing them out for talking behind my back, marching over there and bulling my way in. But right now, there's not much else I feel like doing other than standing here.

"Okay, we've got some ground to cover." Cieran's voice cuts through the murmurs that I've tuned out again.

This time, I'm more focused, moving without hesitation when the others do. Forcing my limbs into motion. Since we'd stopped, I'd started losing reasons to keep moving.

Silence falls among us for the most part, broken only by faint curses at missteps in the shale, calling out some holes just waiting to snag an ankle. The rock changes, turning a rustier red, breaking into large boulders among scrawny trees and clumps of cacti.

The ground starts to fall into ravines, displaced debris from our boots rattling down the side if we get too close. Some gorges spin out into wider canyons where rainwater has aggressively chiseled at the rock.

Cieran leads us carefully, picking the best paths across the undulating ground. Trees start to get larger, the ground a little steeper. One hand wave and silence falls, boots stepping more carefully as we make our way up to the top of the canyon wall.

We came from the north side, where plenty of trees and brush give us cover and spread a welcome bit of cool. Red rock canyon spreads out below, sheer sides peppered with caves and a linked dwelling system once used by native tribes long ago. We sink down in a loose line, keeping cover and making sure there's no glint or rustle to give us away.

Athina points and I confirm what she sees. A smudge of shadow in a rocky nook. Lookout.

A ladder, made more recently than five hundred years ago, is propped up against the rocky wall, rungs leading up to the openings closest to the ground. At least thirty feet up. It's going to be easy for them to defend that position. We're going to need that ladder.

Remy presses a hand to the ground, eyes closing, and fingertips curling into the soil. His head tilts slightly, forehead creasing.

The officers wait patiently.

"They've laced both entrances with something," Remy finally reports. "But I'm only getting heat signatures for four guards, and three kids."

Cieran and Dimos share a frown. That's way fewer than we're supposed to be finding out here. Maybe the intel was wrong or we're too late.

The buzzing in my head gets louder, and seems to be filling up my ears now. I absently rub my left ear, and the noise muffles.

I can add idiot to the list for today.

Takis lifts his head. He's got good hearing to pick up the sound of that truck.

"Incoming," I mouth, chin jerking to the west. There's a track running through the canyon, wide enough to have been made by a truck just like the two coming down the makeshift road.

"There they are." Satisfaction lines Cieran's voice. Eight men, all human judging from the lack of pointed ears and brightly colored eyes to mark fae or elf heritage, hop out of the trucks and off the back. But doesn't mean there's no warlocks—humans with innate elemental based magic like Remy—or shifters among them. They throw open the doors to the covered beds, and start hauling out kids.

With my elf vision, double that of humans, I can see seven dazed and confused and tear-streaked faces like they're right in front of me. The men all have swords, and at least two have bows, strung and ready to use on any runners. The tips are covered with something blunt and shimmering. Probably just a stunning spell. They could have gotten that off the black market or from a resident warlock.

The kids are hustled to the ladder. Another is lowered from the secondary cave and a couple kids are shoved in that direction. Athina hisses between her teeth, locked in on one of those kids with the same skin coloring as the fleet. Silver glints around his neck, a collar blocking him from shifting into dragon form, if he even can at his age. Her hand flicks toward her throat. She has a faint scar around her neck from a similar collar. Cieran's got a matching scar after they shared the burden of her burning the collar off. He reaches over and squeezes her wrist.

I look again. The rest of the kids all have some sort of magic dampener on as well. Iron laced to block magic or silver to block shifting. That's our confirmation that the traffickers are only going for magic users. The kids slowly climb the ladder, not getting a chance to refuse. Once they're up with most of the guards, those remaining on the ground take the ladders and lay them at the foot of the canyon wall.

Cutting off any escape other than a thirty-foot jump.

It's all done efficiently, practiced many times over. This isn't their first load of kids ferried across the unofficial border that's sprung up between eastern and western states.

But if this mission goes to plan. It'll be their last.

3

Dejan

Athina slips off to scout down the canyon rim, merging with the shadows. I edge a little farther away. It's what I usually do. Find some higher ground, ready to use my bow, keeping elf sharpened eyes and ears out.

The others sink back into the growth. We'll strike in a few hours, once the sun moves farther west and the guards feel safe and secure. The hum grows again, and this time it *is* just in my head.

A hairy spider the size of my palm makes its slow and steady way over the rocks, pauses at my leg, then lifts mottled brown-and-black front legs and continues its march over me. Once it's gone, I lift my head, blinking at the shadows that have shifted on the canyon walls across from me. I've been looking at that damn tarantula for who knows how long instead of keeping eyes out.

A faint crackle in my ear announces Cieran checking in over comms. I glance his way and get the force of his sergeant look. Something I'm not used to seeing. I idly wonder if he knows he has that expression. He usually keeps it informal, but there's an edge that overtakes him on missions. One that we're all glad to see, since he's the one making the calls to get us home or not.

I lift my hand in a slow and pointed motion and tap the comm in my right ear, sending back the "all clear" signal. He doesn't flinch and doesn't really look away until I do.

This time, I keep my focus on the canyon while sneaking glances to my left, keeping an eye on the others, making sure I'm not missing something again. All's quiet. Takis has eyes closed, the gentle rise and fall of his chest deceptively calm. He's not quite asleep, just doing that sort of hover between sleep and awake during the waiting game.

Cieran's still on alert, but his head tilts occasionally. Athina and he are talking through their mental connection. Most heartbonds don't get more than an exchange of feelings, a certainty of the other person. Dragonwalker telepathy apparently extends to heartbonds with humans.

Dimos has a tablet out, sketching across the surface, glancing across the canyon periodically. The guards haven't changed from their initial routes in a thirty-foot square, keeping eyes out around the canyon.

The two-hour mark creeps up. They're starting to get careless. Two have been talking at a corner of their route for three minutes, hands sloppily positioned on their weapons.

I tap twice through the comms. Besim nudges Takis and he sits up, instantly alert. Remy emerges from somewhere and a jolt of surprise runs through me. I'd forgotten about him. Literally out of sight, out of mind.

Cieran and Dimos lay out the plan. I'm not sure when they coordinated it. But I don't really need the comms to hear the muted briefing.

Nods pass around and I tilt a thumbs-up from my position. We don't have full intel of what's in those caves, but that might make things more interesting.

The others disperse along the canyon edge. I get my rope and climbing harness ready, looping it around the nearest tree and giving a tug to test.

Once they're out of sight from the caves, Takis and Iosef will shift long enough to get across the canyon and circle around to flank from above. The others will rappel down to the canyon floor and stealthily make their way back to launch an attack. I'm cover from above. If I can remember.

My hand works in and out of a fist. I *need* to remember. This is too important. My gaze locks on to the caves opposite, finding the guards, running over the plan again and again. But with each reminder, it feels like the droning in my head deepens, trying to overwhelm my attempts to stay in the present.

Hurry up.

Motion at the top of the opposite canyon wall jerks me from a vacantly curious feeling. Shit. I've done it again.

A faint buzz in my ear has me jumping and I'm glad no one is around to see me jolt like a high-strung squirrel.

"Still with us, Dej?" Cieran.

I scowl, hating that it's an accurate question and wondering what they're thinking about me in their various positions. And now I've left him waiting for an answer about five seconds longer than normal. Great. Definitely reassuring that I'm fine.

"Yes, *Sergeant.*" There. That'll help, except I did sort of mean the officer title.

A huff comes across the comms. I'm still okay for now.

"Countdown starts now. Fifteen seconds."

I scowl again, but I did need to be reminded of the timing since half the plan vanished from my memory in the twenty-two minutes it took them to get into position. Clip the rope to my harness, make sure it's still tied off securely. Get an arrow ready to go. Move forward. Sight the first lookout.

Three, two, one.

I loose an arrow and the lookout falls, making way for the figures launching themselves over the cliff's edge and rappelling down.

The first alarmed shout dies to another of my arrows. Cieran appears behind another guard and the man goes down instantly. Another spins right into Dimos and doesn't stand a chance. Someone appears in the left cliff opening, and I fire again, but my arrow slams off something.

Perfect. Shielded.

"Rem, you're up on those openings," I say.

"Already on it," comes his reply.

Takis and Iosef pause halfway down the cliff, antsy where they're hanging out in full view.

The exterior guards are down, but there's more in the caves. A rumble shakes the canyon and vibrates all the way through my feet.

There's a faint *chink* and something cracks at the cave opening. I fire again and this time the figure spins away, arrow in his arm. I frown. That should have been a direct hit.

But we've finally stirred the hornets. Takis and Iosef finish their descent, barely slowing on the ropes and swinging in through the openings. Swords flash and they set in position. The others get the ladders up to both caves, and Remy and Athina each start up one.

Dimos and Cieran are next, leaving Besim and me as rearguards. I fidget, getting bits and pieces through comms and what echoes out of the caves. Finally, Cieran and Athina both appear at separate entrances, shepherding three kids out between them. The kids, painfully and gingerly, turn and start climbing the ladder.

Besim patiently encourages from the ground, waving them on. A rumbling sound comes from the left cave. Athina turns, her posture like hackles are raised. She braces, and gets hits by confusing motion. Then she and Remy are thrown from the cave mouth.

Cieran wrenches around with a surprised cry. Remy's already got a hand out, and their fall slows enough that they aren't a heap of broken bones when they impact with grunts audible from my position on the other side of the canyon. I wince, but still don't move.

Because I'm locked on to what's coming out of that cave. A serpentine nose appears, and sinuous body wiggles out, long claws latching into the rock. The thing scales the side of the cliff and twines around to catch Remy and Athina in its sights.

It's not a dragon, or any kind of shifter I've ever seen. Sickly yellow smoke coils between curving fangs. Athina pulls Remy up by the strap of his vest and they get out of range from the cave mouths. Besim shouts and gestures to the kids. His skin glints grey, the protective stoneskin he inherited from his troll father called up as another layer of armor.

Feedback whines in my ear and I flinch away from it.

"Shoot that thing, Dej!"

Well, I finally managed to piss off Besim. But I'm doing the same thing to myself. I lurch into motion, yanking an arrow out and sighting. It bounces off scales, but draws the thing's attention to me.

Its long and sinuous neck slowly rises and pale eyes lock onto me, even a hundred yards away. A new sort of lethargy spreads over my arms, something urging me to just put the bow down, turn around, and forget everything I ever knew. Swirling yellow is all I can see.

I'm about to do what it suggests, because it's the best idea I've heard all day.

A roar reverberates through my chest. The creature rocks back under a dragonwalker in full black-scaled dragon form clamping onto its neck.

My hands tremble, and I'm looking at them in mystified silence when my name is shouted again.

Cieran has a kid clinging to his chest, arms and legs wrapped around him. The sergeant manages to get another slung over his shoulder. I nock another arrow as he gets a foot on the top rung of the ladder. He positions his hands and feet and slides down the ladder, landing unsteadily on the ground.

Besim is there to snatch the kid from over his shoulder. Athina shouts and scrambles forward, only to be driven back by short spears hurled down from the right cave opening. Takis still fights that *thing* in his dragon form. Shale falls and roars tremor as they scramble along the top of the cliff. Brilliant fire erupts from Takis but the thing doesn't flinch, just launching another hissing attack.

Dimos and Iosef appear in the left tunnel opening, Iosef barely holding the bleeding officer up. Athina moves forward again, this time with Cieran providing cover with his rune-reinforced shield. They don't get far before something is lobbed from the other cave. Cieran pushes her back and, when the wildfire grenade explodes, they're only caught in the percussive blast, a bit of fire catching at her sleeve.

My arrows ping off a new blocking spell. Besim shields the kids on the canyon floor with his body. They're crying and screaming where they huddle against some rocks. Three more figures have appeared at the openings, pressing Iosef hard from his posture and the fire spilling from his outstretched hand. He doesn't have room to shift in the cave.

Cieran gets back to Athina, and they both curl under his shield again as they retreat. I try a few more arrows. At least the figures flinch away from the arrows, maybe not quite trusting the barrier. Either way, it gives the crew time to regroup.

Remy shouts and Dimos starts to pull his way to the ladder. Cieran joins Remy and they creep forward a few steps, Cieran taking the brunt of the weapons and shimmering magic bolts raining down against the shield surface. Most bounce off, some skim back to leave smeared burn marks against the rocks. The dwarven developers are sure earning their paychecks with those shield upgrades.

"Keep them busy Dej." Cieran's voice is accompanied by a grunt.

Remy's hands spread, his left hand hits his chest, then he thrusts out, one palm up, the other perpendicular where his wrists touch. I shake my head, snapping a few more arrows off. I'm about out. Remy needs some time to drag Dimos down and catch him. If he's feeling stupid, he's probably trying to catch the still-fighting Iosef in the same area of affect and yank him from the caves too.

Another roar announces the creature shaking off Takis. The dragonwalker tumbles from the air, tail whipping and wings beating to get his feet under him and land in billows of dust. The creature skitters on the cliffside, peering down and trying to catch someone in its look.

Dimos flails ungracefully, Remy guiding him down. Takis takes the captain under his wing. Iosef jumps, landing on his fleetmate's back. I grab the line connected to my harness and slam the bow into the holster on my back. A running start and I'm rappelling down the cliff, barely slowing because that's how I'd get shot.

My knees twinge when I hit ground and spin behind a rock. I whistle and the comforting whine of intact arrows returning to the quiver sounds. I hold...three, two, one. Then grab my bow again and take an arrow from the nearly full quiver. A glance shows the fleet and my crew retreating. They still hold a loose line, under as much cover as they can, but we're about to get pinned down for certain.

The thing scrambles closer, more bits of rock tumbling from the cliff. An unfamiliar dragon bursts from the cave, scales almost black with a purple sheen to them. Oh, that's going to piss four dragonwalkers off.

I check the distance, and at Besim's wave, sprint over to them. Heat chases me to his side. It cuts off as Remy throws a blue-tinted magic shield up, sweat beading his forehead and dripping down his cheeks. He's going to need a break from using his magic *soon*.

Takis has shifted back and he favors his right leg. Dimos needs immediate medical aid but I'm just staring at him, fascinated by the dripping red.

"Dejan!" Hands drop on my shoulders, and I'm jerked to look into Cieran's eyes. Remy grunts as another round of enemy dragonfire and a few wild magic grenades drop against his shield.

"We need a medic."

Medic.

That's me.

Shit.

I should be calling healing magic from my hands, should be pulling my med kit from its detachable place underneath my pack. But I'm just standing there, back to looking at the blood like I'm just a kid and unaware that I could do anything to help with my magic. Forgetting twelve years of paramedic and Army medic experience.

Cieran curses, and Dimos is turning an alarming shade of pale. I try to cover, starting to find the med kit, but it's like fumbling in the dark.

Iosef kneels by Dimos. He's helped me out before in the field, on Cieran. But I don't think he's got the right kind of magic.

"What do you need?" he asks, and I'm not about to just stare at a dragonwalker.

"Uh…a stretcher." My mind starts to turn, creaking and grinding like wheels breaking free of rusting ice. I finally coordinate getting the med kit, and pull out bandage packs. "Get these on the worst spots."

Iosef does as ordered, placing pressure on the bleeding gashes on Dimos's right leg. His right arm's not looking much better. The breastplate has scratches across the side, but nothing punctured through.

"We need to get out of here!" Besim has a kid trying to crawl into his pack.

Cieran checks the sky, but that thing still skitters around, spitting smoke and acid. The dragon circles, flames spouting and bursting.

The sergeant's brow creases, and he looks to Remy. "We need an out, Rem."

Remy shakes his head. "I'm not good enough at it, Sarge."

"We don't have an option. Just get us far enough we can regroup."

"I'll have to drop the shield." Remy looks sick to his stomach. He's terrible at portal gates or transport circles. It takes too much magic, no matter how he practices. Fire magic isn't quite right for portals or gates. It can be too volatile. Air- or Earth-based magic is. Or fae, the way they draw magic right from their surroundings like sponges, something about their DNA and Gaelic language acting as a refinery. But we don't have any of that kind of magic here, just Rem's.

"I'll cover." Iosef pushes the gauze back at me and muscle memory kicks in, my hands working almost of their own accord. I dump coagulation powder on the gaping slashes on Dimos's thigh. If this doesn't slow the bleeding in the next five seconds, I'll have to tourniquet. My magic should have been first line of defense but that's been another issue in the last three months.

"How long?" Cieran asks.

Remy waits until Iosef's magic spreads like a blanket over us to answer. "Two minutes."

Athina kneels next to me, her hands joining mine in applying pressure to wounds on Dimos's arm. Her eyes sear over me, making sure I'm going to actually take care of her fleetmate.

Iosef's hold isn't as strong as Remy's, and we duck a few times at the hammering magic. One pass has heat curling at my ears.

"Rem!" Cieran doesn't really have to urge Remy faster. Even the kids have shut up, seeing that our warlock is putting everything he's got into spinning a portal gate. He's prepping as well as he can, anchoring his magic to his center with moves drawn from the Hawaiian Ha'a, but he's going to be wiped out even if he can get it to work.

Two minutes creep, and Dimos isn't moving too much but everything's packed with gauze and wrapped tight with bandages. My bloody hands tremor slightly. They haven't done that since my first call years ago, one that had even my veteran partner a little white. If we don't get out, Dimos might not make it. And that's going to be on me.

"I won't be able to hold it long," Remy grits out. He spreads his hands and a shimmering, swirling circle opens up against the rock, showing a differing landscape of scrub-dotted hills on the other side.

"Bes, get the kids." Cieran beckons Takis and they step through to check safety. Cieran returns in a second, helping Athina pull Dimos up. I scramble, holding back for them to get through first. Then Besim is practically tossing kids through the portal.

Remy slams to one knee, arms shaking as he holds the portal open. I pause. I need to do something, say something, but my hands dangle uselessly at my sides.

"I'm last through," he strains.

I walk through, and there's a faint buzz in my head that says I should have argued or stayed. Iosef lurches through and then Remy appears. A bit of fire chases after him before he drops the connection and the portal seals off.

He collapses in front of me, unable to get himself upright. I stare at him, not even moving as he loses the bit of lunch he still had in his stomach over one of my boots. A low curse follows, and he tries to move, arms shaking.

A hand jams into my chest and knocks me backward. "You gonna help him or just stand there like a *firren* lawn ornament?" Cieran growls, scooping a hand under Remy's arm and hauling him up. I slowly move, reaching out to help steady him. Remy's dark skin is concerningly pale, pupils dilated, and his boots shift all over like he's not sure how to stand.

Shock. Adrenal overload. Too much magic all at once.

He needs something.

What?

I know this.

His tac vest. Emergency chocolate bar in the front pocket farthest to the right.

I grab it, and peel back the wrapper. Remy hangs off Cieran, who's going a little red trying to support Remy's dead weight. Besim appears, pulling Remy up taller. I tip Rem's head back and shove the chocolate in his mouth, hand against his chin, holding his jaw shut.

It takes a second before the sweetness tinted with a healing charm hits him and he flinches. Then he's chewing, grimacing because like some heathen, he doesn't like chocolate. Even if it's his son's favorite.

Cieran keeps hold of him as he steadies. Besim heads back to help Iosef carry Dimos. Athina gives room and starts shepherding the kids into a group. Shock and fear still cover their faces. Faint sobs still come from a few of them.

"The...the rendezvous should be just ahead." Remy's hand wobbles forward. Idiot. He didn't just get us out of range, he got us over fifty miles away to where we were supposed to have flown with the shifters.

"Dej, take point."

"Yes, sir." It comes automatically.

Cieran narrows his eyes. "Since when do you call me *sir*?"

Even blurry, confused Remy looks at me like I've suddenly got horns. I turn and jog up the hill, remembering barely to get out my bow.

Sure enough, once I top the low rise ahead, there's a small collection of transportable buildings set up inside a six-foot-high chain-link fence. We established a meetup here with the Bureau of Magical Affairs once we had rescued kids. It's some sort of border humanitarian camp, run by civilian doctors, helping take care of refugees over the Mexican border from whatever civil war they've got going currently between territories. Perfect for us to crash into with our injured soldiers and rescued kids who'll need some friendlier faces other than us.

We stumble down the hill. I fall back, taking Remy without a word, but Cieran still gives me that look. My charade is over and I'm going to have to come clean. If I don't blank out again between now and then.

The kids perk up, and Athina somehow manages to keep all four in a line with Takis limping alongside. She's got a smaller one on her back. Dimos is flagging, drooping lower and lower between Besim and Iosef.

Cieran jogs ahead to reassure the camp guards and get a med team on standby. They wave us through. Two more fall in with us, leading the way to the biggest building.

We step inside. An elven doctor in light green shirt tucked into faded jeans, serviceable boots, and a white coat and stethoscope around her neck comes to greet us. But as soon as I clock her face, I almost drop Remy.

Tara?

And the part of my heart that I had magically removed fifteen years ago, *twinges.*

4

TARA

My greeting dies. I knew a team would be coming in with rescued kids, probably some wounded. But I didn't know it would include *him*.

Damn it.

He stares at me like he's seeing a ghost, and I know I'm not looking much better. At least until the anger rushes in and I snap back to the present. I tear my gaze away from those silver-green eyes, ignoring the way his blond hair is a little unruly and definitely not strict military style under a backwards ballcap. Since when does he wear those?

My heart can't betray me, since he destroyed our heartbond years ago.

The human in front of me eyes me warily. He's in dark fatigues, some sort of hooded jacket under an armored vest and neck protection. These guys don't look like regular border patrol. Then I clock the Drax Guard patch.

Ah. Don't mess with them.

"Sergeant Cieran O'Donnell." His voice is raspy and hoarse. Dirt and smoke smudge across his face and armor, and the other soldiers standing around him look about the same level of beat. Except for the one about to bleed out and the other that *De'janick Kostic* is supporting.

"Doctor Tara Novak. Let's hold the pleasantries until we get him patched up." I point at the injured man. Actually. Not man. He's from a different unit or squad or whatever they call themselves. And I can almost taste the shifter magic around them.

"Good plan." Cieran waves and all the soldiers churn to motion. I direct the injured shifter to the cordoned-off surgical area where we keep a sterilized table and instruments ready at all times. The two men supporting him lay him down and get to work stripping armor and weapons.

I stop a nurse as she rushes by. "Angie, check the kids. Triage if needed."

She nods and changes course. One of the soldiers is a woman, and she stands protectively in front of the kids. She'd probably break some hands without blinking. But once Angie introduces herself, the woman helps steer the kids through the door to the next interconnected building away from impending surgery.

The sergeant helps support the other Drax soldier. But he's moving and there's no blood to be seen. I'm *not* going over there.

"He just needs to lie down," Cieran says. "Dej can help you with Dimos."

Dej looks almost pleadingly at his sergeant, but he doesn't need to worry.

"I've got people I can depend on to help me." And I stalk over to the surgical area to start prepping.

I thought I'd put the past behind me, moved on as best I could with a hole in my heart. Actually, more than one. Because the one thing worse than feeling the heartbond suddenly vanish was learning that De'janick was still alive, that *he'd* had it removed, and had disappeared two days after my dad was arrested for being connected to the Kostic drug clan. Organized crime De'janick had never explicitly *said* he wasn't involved in. Stupid, naïve me, too in love with the elf who'd seen some of my dreams that I kept hidden from everyone.

I guess he decided I wasn't worth it after he left town to dodge the fallout of his family's organization being gutted by the Feds.

Raquel, my human assistant for the last four years, arches an eyebrow as she slides surgical gloves over my hands, and then ties the gown behind me.

I don't say anything, letting her adjust my mask, before stepping up to the table.

"Get fluids and find a vein," I order even though another nurse is already on it. "Let's see what we've got." At my nod, Raquel cuts away the first bloody bandage on his thigh and I start assessing. The two soldiers are still there. I glance to the one who has similar gear to my patient.

"Tell me about him."

Raquel irrigates the wound, and I pick up needle and thread to start the first round of stitches.

"Dragonwalker. Thirty-two. Has a copper stay down his left ribs."

Raquel glances at the identification tags around his neck and confirms. The man's eyes flicker and a hoarse sound comes from him. His sats are falling with continued blood loss. Fates, I do *not* want to know what caused this. It takes the nurse a couple tries to get an IV in, and he gets some fluids started along with pain meds.

"Get him on some oxygen. And I want meds first before we push any magic."

The second nurse whirls to get oxygen set up. Copper stay. That's to keep magic *in*. I glance at the man. The tags are barely visible where they've slipped off his shoulder to the table. *Dimos Kostas.*

I've got one powerful shifter on my table.

"Blood type?" Though I doubt we have any dragonwalker blood in our emergency cabinet. Blood transfusions work best between shifters of the same type. Same with magic users, or other races.

The dragonwalker soldier doffs his bracer and rolls up his sleeve in response. "I'm universal donor."

"Got it." I turn to our young elf resident. "Andrew, get—"

"Iosef," the soldier supplies.

I incline my head, curving the needle through skin again. Something pokes up through the skin. A silver scale trying to protect Dimos from the tiny punctures each pass of the needle brings. We might need a suppressant, so his body doesn't try to shift mid-surgery.

"Get Iosef set up. We're going to need at least two bags."

Iosef takes a seat and clenches a fist, sending veins popping on a muscled forearm.

"Then keep monitoring vitals for me."

I settle into the work, alternating with Raquel on stitching, wiping, irrigating, giving a quick pass of healing magic, before she follows up with bandages. Letting it fill my mind instead of thinking on my ex out there somewhere.

Dimos is going to have one hell of a headache once he comes to. And De'janick better have one hell of an explanation once I muster the courage and calmness to stand face-to-face with him for the first time in fifteen years and demand answers.

5

DEJAN

REMY CRASHES ONTO A cot, eyes already closed by the time he hits the pillow. Cieran hefts Rem's feet up onto the cot and unbuckles the sword belts, pulling at the weapons and Remy's vest to get them off. The warlock grumbles, one hand half-lifting to try to swat in annoyance.

Cieran turns on me next. Besim comes over. They both looked pissed. Takis and Iosef glance my way and their expressions worm to the back of my mind to sting.

"Sit down," Cieran growls. Athina is wearing off on him.

I obey, taking the cot a few feet from Remy. Cieran blinks in surprise at my lack of fight. It's getting harder to do anything other than follow direct commands. It's only by focusing on his face that I'm keeping the roaring noise at bay and staying in the present.

He jams arms across his chest, but then turns away, head shaking. "Stay put. Bes, keep an eye on them. I'm headed out to scout. You've got until I come back to have a really *firren* good explanation, *Corporal.*"

Okay. That one pricks too.

"Cir." Besim nudges his arm, but our sergeant moves away, a sharp urgency around him.

Athina barely pauses Cieran from his mission. "I'll go with you," she says.

"No, I'll see if I can borrow a truck."

She huffs, hands finding her hips. "Don't be stubborn. I'll get us there quicker."

"Fine." It's short and sharp and then he strides out. Athina glances at us, but I've definitely got nothing. Besim maybe gives some sort of reassurance before she hurries after Cieran.

My gaze falls to my hands still bloody from working on Dimos. They're limp and rest palm up on my thighs. I should be calling up green-tinted magic, checking Remy. Helping figure out if the kids are okay. Helping with Dimos.

But it's just my lightly tanned skin and calloused fingertips.

"Dej." Besim crouches by the cot. He's tall enough for it to still put us almost eye-to-eye with me sitting on the low surface. "Talk to me."

"I..." Tremors rock through me. It takes staring at him, this giant of a man, and glancing over at Remy passed out on the cot because he'd done his damnedest to get us all out while I'd just stood there, something I swore I'd never do again, to finally admit, "I'm not right anymore, Bes."

I've known them both for almost five years. My three years in the Army before had just been a stopover, a place for me to get used to the military before testing into the Drax Guard. But these two, our old sergeant, they'd become family, brothers somewhere along the way. Cieran's starting to. I never told them as much, but I think they know.

His hand closes over my shoulder, gently rocking me. "It's that spell?"

I nod. Fates, I've never really let him use his gentle, therapy tone on me without a token fight. I must really be messed up.

"Shit." It sort of sobs from me. "I can't...I'm gonna get you all killed."

"Hey, that's a pretty quick jump." He doesn't let up.

Maybe it's the contact, or someone finally really knowing, but it's a little easier to say, "I don't know, you're pretty helpless."

Faint amusement spears across his broad features. "What do you need, Dej?"

My hands curl into fists. A lot of things. My gaze flits away, finding Tara's silhouette across the room in the surgical area. And not having her around is one of them.

On second thought, maybe I'm glad I'm losing all feeling, because facing off with her is going to go even worse than me admitting I'm compromised to my team.

Besim gently nudges me, and I recover, focusing on him. "Talk Rem off the cliff when Cieran gets back."

Wry understanding crinkles around his eyes. "Yeah." He tilts a glance at the unconscious warlock. His hand lifts from my shoulder to scrub across his jaw. "Hearing this is gonna hit him hard."

"I thought you were encouraging me."

Besim chuckles and taps my knee with a fist. "We can talk about that doctor?"

I'm definitely still in my right mind enough to glare. A louder laugh shakes his shoulders, and he pushes to his feet. "I'm going to find some coffee. You want any?"

"Sure."

He's leaving me despite what Cieran said. Chances are high I'm not moving from this cot anyway. But he still arches an eyebrow and I nod. I'm not getting him into trouble.

I'd always been alone. In the regular enlisted forces, it was easier to keep distance between the other soldiers and myself as the medic. I'd thought I could do the same once I made it into the Guard. But there's no room for distance in a crew. Not with the types of missions we run, and not with being paired with Remy and Besim, two men who are completely open and honest. My past experience with people like that had been "honesty" until they got what they wanted, or turned to start manipulating you in some way.

So I set out to make them show their true colors as fast as possible, not interested in wading through the bullshit until they did.

Except they'd already been showing me. Besim's Catholic, faithful, and you know he means it when he prays for you. Hell, I've seen the good come of his prayers firsthand. Ten years ago, I'd have been vehemently against it, but after just a few months of knowing Besim, I changed my attitude. Now I'm secretly relieved when he pulls out his rosary and starts praying. There's not much you can do to piss him off. He's got seven siblings and he's as steady as a mountain. Could probably move one with his faith. He's patient enough to try it.

Remy can't tell a lie to save his ass. He's an incredibly powerful warlock. Something else that kept me ill at ease around him at the start. In Detroit no one had that kind of magic without plans and muscle to back it up. He kept being friendly no matter what. Sometimes with obviously gritted teeth. Until I didn't listen on a mission and recklessly went ahead. I triggered a trap, and only Remy's reflexes saved the two of us from being obliterated. When the magic stopped, he punched me in the face. I deserved it. And it finally made me realize that he'd save me again with no expectations and had no motivation for using his power other than to protect and serve. So I fixed his dislocated shoulder, and we didn't say anything more about it.

Our old sergeant was the same way. Pothos is a strong air warlock, gruff, and expects you to do your job. I'm technically a few years older than he is, but maturity wise, closer to Remy's twenty-seven. Honestly, sometimes when you put Rem and me together, the maturity level drops further. But somewhere along the line, Pothos and I became friends.

Once I got my head on straight, I learned what it was like to have friends, brothers, and surrogate family, since they didn't hesitate to bring me over to dinners with the full Antilles crew or Remy's parents and son. Being trusted immediately with Remy's kid hit me right in the heart. And that's why I've been pushing myself for this long. I can't just abandon them after they've given me so much.

I don't know how long Besim's gone, but it's long enough for me to check out and jump when he's back and holding out a mug of coffee. He doesn't flinch or stare at me weirdly, but he's definitely assessing.

"You gonna take off your pack?" He sips, watching me over the rim of his mug.

I set the mug on the ground and start shrugging out of my weapons harness and pack. I grab a disinfecting wipe and finally clean off my bloody hands. A pointed look down has me reaching for the coffee cup, whose existence had already been erased.

I clear my throat, leaning on my knees, and cup my hands around the mug. "The kids okay?" They'd been moved to some other building pretty quick.

"From what I can tell." He divests his own pack and longsword.

"Good."

He groans a little as he sits in a folding chair and stretches his legs out. Coffee scalds down my throat. It's genuinely horrible, but my body doesn't even muster a reaction. Besim lets the silence linger. That's something that made me instantly comfortable around him years ago. He saw my silence and didn't try to force conversation.

Some point later, a muffled groan and slow movement announces Remy waking up. He partially curls up, hand dragging up to scrub at his eyes.

"Caffeine?" It's a barely decipherable mumble as his eyes crack open.

Besim chuckles and pushes to his feet. He reaches over to tap Remy's shoulder. "I'll get some now."

A sound like a waking Vinland mammoth comes from Remy, and he tucks further on his side like he's about to pass out again. I note in mild surprise that my mug is still mostly full and now a barely palatable temperature.

"Doing okay?" One of Remy's bleary eyes appears over the cot's edge.

I nod, looking away. "Yeah. You?"

"I feel like shit."

"You look it," Besim cheerfully announces as he returns with another cup of coffee.

Remy's apparently exhausted enough still to not flip the half-troll off. Just starts pushing himself upright, groaning like he's nearing three hundred years, neck popping as he tilts his head side-to-side. He rolls the shoulder he's been lying on and it cracks. Besim patiently waits as the warlock scrubs his hand through the hair now sticking up in unruly waves, and pulls another chocolate bar out of the pocket of his discarded tac vest before taking the coffee.

Remy takes one sip and lurches forward, gagging and spitting it out into the cup. "That's disgusting! What the hell?"

A faint sound rumbles in my chest, echoed louder by Besim. Remy glares at him. "This is the worst excuse for coffee ever."

"They had some tea bags."

"Fates, they've probably ruined that too." Remy hands the coffee back to Besim, who drinks it like it's nothing.

"There's something wrong with you." Remy shakes his head and unwraps the bar.

Boots announce Cieran returning, looking a little windblown and exhausted. Athina is with him, rubbing her shoulder under the strap of her breastplate.

"Coffee?" he says hopefully.

"Don't do it," Remy mumbles through a bite of chocolate. Besim hands the cup. Cieran takes a sip, shrugs, and goes for more.

"It's got a nice burned flavor." Our sergeant finally shudders, one eye twitching as the bitterness really hits him. Athina shakes her head, takes the mug, tries it, and her eyes flash a bright copper.

"No." She spins away. "I have coffee in my bag for you. I'm making a round."

"I love you." He looks at her with pure adoration. Hopefully I never looked like that.

But it's gone when he turns back to me and the sergeant returns. I swallow hard. Cieran takes the chair and Besim sinks down beside Remy, who makes some space and sends a tenuous glance at the cot to make sure it's going to hold both of them.

"I...uh..." I hate that this is erasing every bit of confidence I ever had. "They call it 'stoneheart.'"

Cieran sits back, gaze cutting into me. "They told me they didn't know what was wrong with you."

My hands are fists again. "I told them not to tell." Technically it's my health information and not a free-for-all.

"Dejan."

Well, this is not making him any less pissed.

"I didn't want any of you to know. I thought maybe it wouldn't be that bad." Ha.

"It's getting worse," Besim states calmly. Remy curls in on himself. The thoughtful way Bes watches me just tells me that he's at least suspected since the beginning, and that computer savvy brain of his is collecting more data points from what I said to match how I've been for the last few months. I should have known Besim had noticed, and was probably just waiting for me to say something since that's what we do—he waits, and I eventually talk because Besim always has an answer. But this time, I knew he wouldn't.

"Yeah." I clear my throat. "It's covering up my heart, hardening around it somehow without stopping function." Yet. "But it's more than that. I'm...I'm losing feeling, emotions. Hell, I'm losing time. I just check out and just sort of exist until someone talks to me."

"Why didn't you say anything? You could have compromised every-thing." Cieran's voice rises.

I swivel to him, something like anger stirring deep inside. "Because I couldn't just turn my back on you all. I had to keep trying until..." Until I had to walk away.

A noise breaks, and Remy pushes up, horror in his eyes. "This is—"

"Not your fault." Emotion breaks through and for a blessed moment I can *feel* again. "I'm not apologizing for stopping that *crytch* from hitting you with this. It's taking everything from me, Rem. She would have used it to control you, take more from you. I wasn't going to let that happen." I'm on my feet. He leans back from me and because he can't lie, I see the truth in his eyes. He's known something is off with me and hasn't said anything, to me or anyone else, because he still thinks this is his fault.

"You can't take responsibility for this. You're safe. The crew's safe. And that's all that matters."

I shove past Cieran, and none of them make a move to stop me. But the sight of Tara pulls me up short. Her hands dangle by her sides, lips parted in surprise, maybe horror. She's heard everything from a few feet away. Probably coming over to confront me for the mistakes of my past.

But the coldness rushes back over me, freezing me. Once just knowing she existed filled me with heat, but there's nothing now. I can almost feel the spell coating my heart squeezing tighter, trying to do its job and smother everything even though its caster is dead and gone.

"De'janick?" Her soft voice holds only question and none of the anger I'd seen earlier.

Creaks announce my crew turning to see why I've halted in the midst of storming off, and why she's here, saying a name they don't quite know.

But I can't stay. Can't face another thing. And some self-loathing sneaks through as I escape the building before I lose myself again.

6

TARA

I WATCH DE'JANICK LEAVE. Some small, stupid part of me wants to go after him. Maybe it wouldn't devolve into arguments like it always did in the past.

The rough sound of a throat clearing has me turning. Sergeant O'Donnell is on his feet, arms crossed. He and the others look at me, stony expressions demanding answers.

I'd learned some hard lessons over the years on how to stay calm and cool, harnessing runaway emotions. Med school and then starting up this organization after a few years in hospital practice didn't leave much room for flying off the handle any time I wanted. But all that practice runs away with a sarcastic laugh in the face of those glares.

They want to know if I've hurt *Dejan* in any way. Or maybe mad that I overheard some private conversation. Well. I've known him longer than they have.

I stride over, hands curling up at my sides and squeezing three times before I relax. The sensory feedback helps center my brain back on what I need to do. The warlock still looks shaky, but it might also have to do with what De'janick shouted at him.

"Can I check you over?" I ask.

The tallest soldier looms over me, assessing, and I stare evenly back. He has to be half-troll from the height and broad build. And he's not the first giant of a man to try to intimidate me into a better diagnosis than the one I've given.

Something friendly cracks his scarred features and he steps aside. The warlock sits back down and gives permission with a bare nod. The sergeant still glares in my periphery, but I wait for him to make the first move.

I reintroduce myself and get the warlock's name. Specialist Remy Kalama.

"I'll be pulling my elven healing magic in to help with the assessment," I inform Remy, the routine words calming me. I know what I'm doing.

"Okay." But he still leans back slightly as a light silver-green sheen coats my hands. I verbalize each step along the way before placing hands on his neck, assessing pulse and blood flow. Fingertips to his temples to reduce some of the pounding headache. That gets a relieved exhale. Then hand hovering above chest to get as much of a read as I can through the armor to check rhythms and tell him what he probably already knows. His magic is going to take time to replenish after whatever he did to almost completely drain it.

Remy's pupils dilate briefly and he braces against the cot until my hand moves away from his chest. The response confuses me. I wasn't even touching him that time.

He instantly relaxes as soon as I step away, his hand brushing his chest before shrugging like nothing shook him up for a second. "Thanks, Doc."

The sergeant blocks my way. My arms cross defensively, mirroring his pose. Let's just get this over with. "What do you want to know?"

"What's up with you and *De'janick*?" Cieran's almost got the Slavic accent for the name, and I'm a little impressed.

"We knew each other fifteen years ago." There's a lot of other things welling up, but I clamp my lips shut. It's not fair to unload them all on his crew and not directly on him.

"And?" Cieran presses.

I shove my curling hands into my white coat pockets, clenching hard. *And* nothing. "He completely betrayed me and my trust. He does it to everyone."

My life had been infiltrated by anyone that De'janick had known—mostly bad—trying to find him after he skipped town. But I was reeling from the betrayal during the minutes I was conscious in a hospital bed. I didn't know anything more than they did.

"He's not like that." Remy pivots on the cot, but his shaking legs make him rethink trying to get up and punctuate the near-harsh assertion.

I scoff. "You haven't known him for long enough then."

"Almost five years," the half-troll says quietly.

My heart twists. If that's true, they've actually known him longer than I did.

The woman soldier returns, carrying mugs by the handles, two in each hand. She wordlessly distributes. When she hands the last to Cieran, they share a look and she leans into his shoulder. His head tips toward hers, and my heart twinges.

"You two have a heartbond." It whispers from me. Jealousy, sadness, regret, *missing*. It all fills up those words. And they both look to me. The sergeant guarded, and the woman with a piercing look.

"You have one with Dejan," she says quietly, that same crisp accent over the harder syllables as the rest of her team.

"Had." I clear my throat. "Before he cut it out fifteen years ago."

And just like that, the anger returns, and I march away. I'm going to find him, and he's going to explain everything.

7

Tara

The thin wooden door slaps shut behind me and I squint in the late afternoon brightness. Dust stirs under my boots as I halt, hands on hips, and force a breath. Our little compound barely stirs. New Mexico State military didn't want to shell out for some security, so I'm paying a private firm for a couple guards to make sure our supplies stay safe, and that smugglers or cartel runners don't come after the refugees in the buildings across from me.

I should check on the kids. Do anything really to avoid talking, or yelling, at De'janick. Looks like he's done me a favor, because he's nowhere to be seen.

My eyes squeeze closed. *Don't think about it.* If he's anything like he used to be, he's going to find a quiet, maybe a high place, and hang out. *Do I really need to talk to him?*

Hands pressing a little harder against my sides, I groan, and turn. I do if I'm going to keep seeing him around for however long they'll be here. There's no high places, but I do know of a few good quiet nooks. And the first is right around the corner.

Favor's gone. He's right there, sitting on the bench in the shaded area between two buildings. I wasn't expecting him there, so I freeze, a lot of different things whirling inside. But before I can retreat, he looks up.

"Hey." He winces. "Hi. Did you want to…I'll leave if you…" He's halfway up, and I've never seen him so unsure.

And his damn voice is worming back, reminding me of so many things we promised each other in whispers. The way he'd hold me tight and let me cry into his shoulder, his soft "love you, Tare's."

I'm about to lose fifteen years' worth of control. "Sit down." It comes out strangled.

He obeys, and I'm trying not to see all the ways he's changed. The uniform, the tac vest and chain mail, the knives, the hat, the muscle bulk he didn't have last time.

I take up a stance against the opposite building, arms crossed tight, keeping a few feet between us like that's going to help at all.

"Why?" It finally breaks free, strangled and furious and seconds away from tears.

Dejan focuses on his hands, fisting inside one another as he leans on his knees. *And he doesn't look at me.*

"Why?" I lurch a step. "Was I not good enough for you? What didn't you have?" A ragged breath catches. I eventually came to terms with *why* he'd left. I just didn't know why he'd left *me.*

"I'm really sorry, Tare."

"No. Don't call me that."

Another wince lines his lightly tanned features. "I'm sorry. Sorry for what I did." Some other expression flashes in his eyes. "But I'm also not talking about this right now."

"The hell you're not." I'm another step forward, close to getting in his face.

"Tar'amischa, this isn't a good time." He stands but I block his way. I'm suddenly looking at a very pissed off De'janick. But I'm already there.

"So a 'good time' was deciding fifteen years ago to cut out our heartbond? A 'good time' was throwing away two years of being together? Don't 'not a good time' me, because you threw me away, and you're going to answer me for that."

We argued plenty back in the day, heartbond or no, but this time we don't have the access to each other's feelings to cut some of the vitriol. His eyes flash and his fingers twitch like he wants to call up some magic.

He's directly in front of me. "Move."

"No. Not until you explain."

A small part of my mind yells at me to back off and give him some space. The De'janick I knew would be a breath from exploding. I know he won't hurt me, still, somehow. I also know that shouting at him isn't a good way to get the explanations I want. And I don't want to regress back to who I used to be and throw barbed words right back at him, trying to make each other bleed.

He's faster than me, skirting around in the space between me and the wall, striding away. I whirl, ready to go after him. But he stops two steps out into the open, just standing there, hands dangling by his sides. It throws me enough that I pause too. When ten seconds pass and he's still just standing there, I stomp forward, circling around, ready to lay into him again.

"You—" I stop. He looks at me in puzzled curiosity, head tilted, and absolutely no recognition in his eyes.

It kills most of the anger, and I frown. He doesn't say anything, just sort of stares at me.

"De'janick, *what's going on with you?*"

He jolts, a fist pressing to his forehead, and a really creative curse escapes. "Tare...I can't..."

Then he's gone, striding away, and if I still know him at all, heading someplace no one is going to find him. I'm left behind again. This time I'm *not going to cry*. But my body laughs at my mind's attempts to stuff everything back in its box.

"Tara?" Raquel's voice interrupts my mini-breakdown. She stands just outside the clinic door. I swipe a hand under my eyes and focus on her. "You okay?" She reaches out, rubbing my arm, bringing the tears budding back to the surface.

"Yeah. Didn't expect to run into my ex out here is all." I try to lighten the words.

Her lips twist in understanding. "Bad breakup?"

A broken laugh escapes. "Try back-alley heartbond removal by him before vanishing for fifteen years."

"Oh, girl." And she folds me in her arms.

"I'm trying *not* to cry, Raquel." I hiccup through more tears. She just shushes me and rubs my shoulder.

"What do you always tell Angie? It's okay to feel your feelings?"

My forehead presses against her shoulder. "Yeah, but that's for Angie, not me."

Raquel clicks her tongue and pushes me away, keeping hold of my upper arms as I scrub at my eyes.

"You need something?" I ask.

"Yeah, to go punch that guy." She squares up, making fists and scowling. But she practices jujitsu, so it's a threat.

I wipe away the last of the tears. "The only one punching him is me."

"Put me down as the backup." She taps my shoulder. "But I was coming to find you because Dimos is waking up."

I shake my hands out, drawing another breath in and out. "Already?"

"Yeah, I figured you'd want to double-check everything yourself."

"Okay." I let her go first, and we head back into the surgical building.

The Drax Guard soldiers are still grouped together, muttering amongst themselves. Remy sits with an openly guilty look on his face, intensifying as he catches my eyes.

I move past, over to the area where Iosef has a hand on Dimos's shoulder.

"Stay down, Captain." Light frustration fills his voice.

Dimos tries to sit up, but winces with every muscle twitch. The woman stands at the foot of the bed, arms crossed, both she and the other male pursing lips at their captain.

I step up to the side of the bed, opposite Iosef. "Hi, I'm Doctor Tara Novak, and I'm going to have to agree with Iosef here and have you settle down."

Dimos turns a look at me, hazy and confused from all the meds that should have kept him asleep for another hour or more. I tilt my head and give him the *look* reserved for especially squirrely patients as I pull on gloves.

He subsides, blinking almost owlishly, and Iosef chuckles quietly. A faint twitch disturbs the woman's features. The fourth man says something in a language I don't recognize and they all smirk. Dimos grumbles back and chuckles float around. I barely pause from checking the bandage on his upper arm.

"Do I want to know?"

"We will be calling you a dragon tamer," the woman replies, her grin spreading. Dimos raises a hand, and she only laughs again at the gesture he gives. "Ah, he will be fine, Doctor." She gently taps Dimos's lower leg.

I offer a smile and get their names. Athina and Takis. The familiar motions of checking bandages, stitches, and giving notes to Raquel to add to the chart helps steadiness flow back in. I bring up my healing magic and coat every wound with a pass before refastening the bandages. He's healing fast. Shifters already heal faster than other humans, and his power must be off the charts since he's got that copper stay. But it's doing him a huge favor and he'll be up in a quarter of the time between his healing and my magic assist.

Dimos breathes easier when I'm done, and comes even more awake.

"Okay." I ditch gloves and start washing hands in the field sink nearby. "I want another transfusion for you and another round of fluids, but you can at least sit up. This bed's about as comfortable as we've got, so bear with us until I discharge you to the slightly more cushioned cots."

He immediately moves, taking Iosef's and Raquel's help to come into a sitting position. Iosef holds him steady while Raquel raises the head of the bed for him to lean against. The copper glint of a heartbond dampener circles Iosef's wrist and I tear my focus away. Everyone is unintentionally trying to remind me of what I've lost.

Dimos blinks again, combating the lightheadedness that's sure to have caused. "Thank you, Doctor Novak."

I tap his wrist. "You're welcome, Captain. This is Raquel, she'll be around with me to keep an eye on you. Feel up to some food?"

He slowly nods, a wince creasing around his eyes, a hand coming to hover over his ribs.

"But not the coffee." Athina's eyes narrow and I can't help but chuckle.

"Sorry. It's Ben's day in the kitchen and he brought some sort of organic coffee alternate that he insists on making because it's 'better for you.'"

"So you can slowly be poisoned to death?"

Raquel laughs. "I've been trying to stage an accidental 'somehow it all fell in the fire' for months now."

Athina snaps her fingers, and fire flickers. "Tell me when."

"Keep the arson to a minimum, hot stuff," Sergeant O'Donnell butts in. She tosses some look over her shoulder that has him smirking and a pang hits hard. A big part of me really wants to dislike them just because they have a heartbond, but I also like to think I've moved on from such pettiness.

Maybe.

"Hey, Dimos, how we doing?" Cieran moves to the bedside, offering a hand that Dimos clasps.

"What's the status?" Dimos asks instead.

Cieran turns to the dragonwalker team. "He's asking for updates already. He's fine."

This gets another round of laughs and a slight frown from Dimos.

"The Bureau team supposed to meet us here ran into some transportation issues. At least two of their trucks are down with overheated engines, and one with a flat tire. So we'll be around longer than expected." He tilts this to me.

"That's fine." I lie straight through my teeth. I don't care if *they're* here, what I really want is De'janick gone and to forget all about him.

"Thanks. We've also got a few hours to figure out if we're going back for the rest of the kids. By my count, there's five left." He looks to the squad, and past them to his team who followed him over.

"That a question?" Takis shrugs his shoulders. Athina stills and like the rest of her team, there's suddenly something very sharp and dangerous around them.

"Mission objective was for as many kids as we could rescue," Dimos says, and O'Donnell quirks a grim smile.

"Doc, can I talk to you for a second?" he asks, and I really don't think I have a choice to say no. We step aside, letting the soldiers stay around Dimos.

"First, wanted to say sorry for snapping earlier. There's been a lot going on recently." He seems genuinely apologetic.

I stick hands in my coat pockets. "Thanks. And it's okay. No one was expecting old interpersonal drama to crop up here."

Cieran huffs and hooks hands in his vest collar. "Yeah. And that's what I wanted to talk about."

I'd rather not, but my sole consolation is that he doesn't really appear to want to either. At least De'janick's not around to make this worse.

"You just tell me what you need. We'll keep to the opposite of camp if needed. I've only got a fraction here, but we're on your turf. If you want distance from Dej, just let me know."

Okay, well I can't *not* like him now. "Thanks. I don't...I just...I..." Apparently I don't know what I need. A faint groan compresses in my gut, and I shove my fists into the bottom of my pockets before straightening. "He decided he didn't want to talk to me. And, admittedly, I sort of yelled at him, which also didn't help. So what's going on with him?"

A scowl distorts his face. "I thought we didn't know, but *apparently* he's been sitting on the answer. He got hit with a spell a few months back on a mission. It's been...changing him, and it's starting to get bad."

And by bad, it looks more than just *piss off your sergeant by being a stubborn idiot* bad.

"He's talking less than usual, is forgetting things, and says he's 'losing time.' It happened earlier, and..." Cieran sighs, shoulders slumping in a posture adjacent to defeat. "And has been happening for a while now. He just stops until someone says something. He called it stoneheart. Any ideas what that is?"

I shake my head, trying to shut down the part of my mind urging me to pull out my tablet and start searching. He mutters something and it's probably not polite based on the urgency of the troll words.

"We're going to be headed back out shortly. If we can freaking find Dejan," he grumbles.

Dejan is hitting nerves all over the place.

"I'll go," the half-troll interrupts. Well, so much for a private conversation. O'Donnell nods sharply and the soldiers all shift into motion at his signal. They check weapons and cluster around Dimos's bed, giving a short farewell. He doesn't look happy to be stuck there while his team is planning something.

I slide around them, stepping closer to the warlock who's re-strapping his vest. "You probably shouldn't be going either." My hands take up residence in my jacket pockets again.

Remy flashes a smile and even though his features are still lined with fatigue, the expression still sets me at ease. "Don't worry. I crammed as much chocolate as I can stand. By the time we get back out there, I'll be okay."

I arch an eyebrow. "You don't like chocolate?" That feels almost like heresy.

His grin twitches again. It seems like it's never really far from the surface. "Dej doesn't get it either." Just as fast the faintly guilty look comes back, like he's afraid I'll be offended by the mention of *Dej*. They're all really comfortable with the nickname—something he *never* let anyone outside of me use. The few who tried got verbally shut down, or glared at and never tried again.

I forcefully clear my throat. Really, convincingly, pretending not to care. "You've known him for five years?"

Remy's turned cautious, slightly protective. "Yes. He's one of the best guys I've known. Saved my life more than once."

I want to argue like I was there, or can speak to what he's been like in the last five years. I know how much *I've* changed in the last fifteen years, why is it so hard for me to admit that De'janick might have as well? This was the last place I'd expected to see him, and honestly maybe it's the special forces uniform that's the strangest part of it all. The elf I used to know didn't stick his neck out for anyone but himself and me.

"You should—" Remy cuts off, attention snapping from me to the door. I turn, something freezing inside at the sight of the half-troll leading Dejan in by the arm. The odd blank look is back on Dejan's face and he's not resisting.

8

DEJAN

"DEJAN! FINALLY." BESIM SHAKES his head and squeezes down the space between two transport trucks. I jolt, not really remembering climbing up the crates of medical supplies to sit near the tent struts.

Besim stops a foot away, craning his head back to look at me. "Been looking for you. Don't make me climb up there."

I check my watch. I'd started the stopwatch when I'd gotten up here, and last I remember, it had just rolled over three minutes. It runs past twenty now. *Fir.* I stand, balancing as the crates shift, and hop off the edge, landing lightly on my toes and tapping the timer off.

Besim rolls his eyes. "Come on, Cieran wants us."

I thump the heel of my hand against my chest. "Yeah? How pissed is everyone at me right now?"

"Including or not including Novak?"

My glare should at least cause some sort of physical damage. He tips his head and leads the way out.

I blink and find myself sitting back on the cot in the surgical building. Cieran shouts as Besim tries to calm him down. Nausea is ever-present on Remy's face, and the dragonwalkers have settled into a row of frowning warriors.

How much time did I lose?

"Damn it!" Cieran yanks off his cap, running a hand through his hair before jamming it back on. Athina watches him carefully, arms crossed, but ready to intervene.

"Sergeant…"

"Don't you *firren* 'sergeant' me!" Cieran whirls on me, striding over and jamming a finger in my chest as I shakily stand. "You lied to us, Dej, and now you're a *firren* liability."

"Cir, I—"

He shakes his head. "You lied and put us all at risk."

"Cieran—" Besim tries to interrupt again.

"No."

I've never seen Cieran this pissed, and it's been a long time since anyone was this mad at me. Though this time I deserve all this and more.

"He knows better. This crew is my responsibility and I'm not—" He cuts himself off, not about to say it and further jinx everything.

Not going to lose another crew.

Apology is the last thing he wants to hear right now. I look to Besim, and he thankfully reads my question. "You just completely blanked on the way over. Couldn't get you to respond to anything other than me just grabbing your arm and walking."

"Shit." It softly whispers from me.

Cieran backs off a step. "Athina and I scouted their camp. They'd left the caves, but we've got a trail. We're headed out to try to grab the last of the kids. You're staying here."

Honestly, that stings worse than any curse he could have thrown at me. But I don't have anything to counter with. "Okay."

Maybe he'd wanted an argument, but he just spins away and strides out the door. Besim frowns but he and Remy aren't arguing the decision.

Neither are the dragonwalkers. Heaviness settles in my gut. I'm too much of a liability.

Athina surprises me by coming over.

"Are you all right, Dejan?" she asks.

A humorless smile flickers across my face. "You know I'm not. And he's right to be pissed. You should all be." I dare to look at the others. "Stay safe out there."

Athina knocks a fist against my shoulder, letting it rest for a moment as she nods. Then moves off. Her fleet does the same, then Besim is there.

His hand grips my shoulder, and I almost desperately clamp my fingers around his bracer. If they leave, who's going to snap me out of another blackout?

Besim studies me for a moment, maybe finally at a loss for words. "We'll be back." The simple statement reassures me. They're not abandoning me. Not yet.

He leaves and it's just me and Remy. There's a gulf between us that hasn't been there since we were new to the crew and trying to figure each other out.

"I'm serious about earlier, Rem." That much I do remember. "I don't regret saving you from this."

"I know." He's a muted version of himself these days, and the faintest frustration rises at that. "Doesn't stop me from blaming myself."

"You shouldn't. I've had your back for years. There's no other place I was going to be than on that mountain helping you get Bear back." I *need* him to understand that. Need him to know that he's the closest thing I've got to a brother, and I'd do anything for him.

He's not quite looking at me, jaw working as he's maybe trying to find words. When he finally returns my look, there's a brighter glint in his eyes and a thickness to his voice when he says, "I know."

The deep sounds of shifted dragons thud outside. They're about to head out without me, and something like desperation cuts through the buzzing trying to take back over.

"Do me a favor, Rem?"

"Yeah?"

"Ask Alder out sometime."

He rolls his eyes, crosses the space between us, and grabs me in a hug. "Shut up."

I return it just as fiercely, desperate for the connection that quiets the humming. And for him to set his sights forward. "And stop blaming yourself. This one is solidly on Ballagh."

Remy pulls back, nodding, but I hold on a bit longer. My heart feels heavier, and the forgetting is creeping back in with its humming drone.

I gently tap the side of my head against his. "Look out for each other out there."

He claps my shoulder. "Don't get too comfortable here. When we get back, we're figuring out how to beat that." He points to my chest, and I muster a faint smile.

If it gets him out the door in the right headspace to take care of the crew, then I'll let him believe there's a cure.

Because I haven't found one.

And believe me, I've looked.

9

TARA

I CAN'T HELP BUT look over my shoulder as Remy strides toward Besim and De'janick. And then I'm staring, watching the almost panic around the sergeant and the team. Something uncomfortable twists inside at the way De'janick blinks and seems more aware, much like outside earlier. My hands clutch my tablet, pressing it to my chest as Cieran shouts and Dejan tries to answer. Then the sergeant leaves, and one by one, the dragon shifters follow. But I'm still stuck, watching the half-troll tap Dejan on the shoulder, some understanding passing between them. Then Remy.

I can't believe my eyes when Dejan *hugs* the warlock. He never does that. Never *did* that.

I almost take a step back from the sight. I was the only one who could get near enough to make physical contact. De'janick always moved through crowds and interacted with people with a space around him. Either physically or with words that held a sharp undercurrent. But I haven't seen that here. Haven't seen him do anything but look at his team with trust, and now with regret as Remy strides out the door and leaves him standing there.

For a moment, I think he's blanked out again, until he pulls his hat off and almost ferociously jerks a hand through his short hair. I definitely hear the curse before he crams it back on his head. Backwards. This hat thing is almost throwing me just as much as the personality shift.

"That's a bad word," a young voice pipes up.

Dejan starts and looks down to his right. He moves enough for me to see a small fae climb out from under a cot.

"Yeah, it is," Dejan agrees easily. "What are you doing down there?"

She clutches one of the stuffed animals we keep around for kids who come through and need something to cuddle.

"I had a snack, but some Band-Aids fell off when I washed my hands. I came to ask for some more. But then there was yelling." She almost leans back with the confession.

"Yeah." Chagrin fills Dejan's voice. "Sorry. You okay?"

She nods, still holding the panda bear against her chest, facing out like it might protect her.

"Let's get you fixed up, okay?"

He sits on the cot and pulls his pack over. She leans over the far edge of the adjacent bed and watches as he gets a small kit out.

"I've got purple dinosaurs or sparkly cats."

I'm still in shock. Even with his back to me there's some different softness to him. I can't remember him ever talking to a kid. Can't remember him ever using some tone like that with anyone but me. Can't remember anyone readily entering his space and him letting them.

The girl climbs onto the cot, scooting to the edge to lean over and look at his options. A grin splits her face. "The dinos have tiaras."

A chuckle comes from Dejan and I almost drop the tablet. It's *gleeful*. "They do. Big tough guys really like them. You tough?" he asks.

She scowls and flexes her arms. He chuckles again.

"Toughest face I've ever seen," he says, taking a Band-Aid and setting his bag to the side. She extends her hand and he applies the bandage. She smiles down at it when it's in place. My heart twists a little. She must have needed some extra healing magic when she came in for her to need Band-Aids. In the case of higher levels of healing magic, the small stuff gets left to heal on its own. I hadn't checked the kids yet, too focused on myself. But my team would have reported if they needed anything else.

"How come you didn't go with the other soldiers?" she asks, still looking at her arm as he gets another out.

Dejan pauses and the air becomes heavy around him for a moment. "'Cause my brain's being kind of silly right now." He applies another. "And sadly, dino Band-Aids can't help it."

She frowns and hops down from the cot. "But you can still protect us, right?"

His shoulders slump a little before he nods. "Yeah." He reaches out to gently tap a fist against her shoulder. "Go play. Keep those dry."

She bounds forward and flings arms around his waist in a hug. Honestly, at this point, I can't predict what he'd do, so him hugging her back for a brief moment doesn't add to the overwhelming shock at this side of him.

"Thank you!" She beams and skips away. He shakes his head slightly as he watches her go, then tucks everything away. And I catch the hint of a whispered curse before he shoves to his feet and steps outside.

I hesitate for a long moment. Then head for the adjacent building that's half extra beds and coffee station and use that exit to reduce the chance of running into him. Get to my office in the next building over and sink into my chair. *Don't do it,* my weary heart tries to argue.

But my jaw juts and I pull my tablet over, flipping it on and starting a search on "stoneheart."

———

My elbows rest on my desk, head in my hands, staring down at the tablet. A few hours of research, a call to a cardiologist friend in Germania who'd been really gracious about me calling after her midnight to bombard with questions, and some files from a colleague over on the east coast, and I don't know what to feel.

Besides mostly sapped of my anger at Dejan. It's easier to call him that and think of him as the soldier than it is to keep thinking about De'janick and all the times we'd had together.

I check my watch. It's well after dinner, and I haven't eaten. I've been in here for at least two hours. Everything must still be running smoothly since Raquel hasn't come to find me for some emergency. The teams aren't back yet. And I have no idea if that's concerning or not.

Don't get involved again. I rub my eyes, tired after staring at the screen for so long. *Don't get involved. The experts have no solution so what do you have?*

I groan and answer my own question. "Overconfidence and a vendetta against him."

The vendetta part is probably not going to help, but my need to start helping in any way possible is trying to roll right over it.

It can't hurt to at least go do some tests?

Like the tests haven't all already been done?

I drop my head to the desk and mumble an "Ow," at the impact. I can't just leave this no matter how much I want to. So I scoop up the tablet and drag my feet across the compound lit by a flaming sunset, halting when

I realize that I have no idea if Dejan is in the main surgical building or not.

But I should probably check in on Dimos anyway. So I keep going.

Raquel meets me at the door. She leans against the wall, biting her thumbnail, as she stares at Dejan. And something that should have been dead and gone inside twinges a little at the sight of him sitting on the cot, leaning on his knees, hands loosely clasped. Alone.

"He's just been…sitting there for hours. I brought some food, but I don't think he even realized I did. It's weirding me out, Tara."

I look closer, catching the vacant look on his face. The tablet taps my forehead and I muffle a groan again.

"What?" Raquel laughs a little.

"I'm going to go get involved."

"Do you want me to talk you out of it? Because I will."

"No. Yes. Ugh, no." I lower the tablet.

"Do I need to punch *you* to knock some sense into you?" She swings around, looking at me with open concern.

"Well. Maybe. Look, it's…" How to distill hours of research? "He got hit with a spell a few months ago, and it's really bad, and…"

"And you want to try to help," she finishes.

"Yeah. Am I stupid?"

"No, you're an empathetic woman with like three degrees and a big heart for the sick and hurting."

I soften and give a smile. "Thanks."

"But if you start making eyes at him, then I will call you stupid." Her grin holds warning.

"You probably don't have to worry about that." Between the unfinished business between us, a missing heartbond, and Dejan's heart turning to stone, me finding any sort of feelings for him again is a slim to none chance.

"You want help? Moral support? An overqualified note taker?"

"Moral support is good." I muster a smile. "I still might want to punch him."

Raquel smirks. "Good." And we head over to Dejan. He doesn't move when we stop in front of him. Barely even blinks. This is weird.

"Dejan?" I ask. And I sort of hate myself as I finally say the shortened form of his name and see it fits this different version of him really well.

But still nothing.

"Kostic?"

Nothing.

Raquel nudges my shoulder and mouths, "*Weird.*"

I don't remember what his rank is supposed to be, so I reach out while somehow still leaning backwards and tap his shoulder. He doesn't even jolt, just sort of looks up at me with a bemused expression. Tracks me as I sit on the cot opposite him.

"Hi."

Just a placid stare back.

Oh this is a mistake. The emotions are starting, and this time it's horror and fury at someone I once knew getting destroyed by a spell.

"Ouch!" I jerk a look to Raquel who gives me a "seriously?" look, fist poised for another punch to my arm.

I clear my throat and straighten my coat sleeve. And try again. Louder. "Dejan."

This time he stirs, blinking hard, and looks around with a deep inhale like he's coming free from underwater. His hand jerks up, going for his face, when he notices me and jolts again. "Shit."

"Yeah, hi," I say wryly.

He checks his watch and looks around again. "*Shit*." This is lower, like I'm not supposed to hear it. "They back yet?" he asks, looking at some point beyond Raquel and me.

"No." My fingers trace around the edge of the tablet. "I've been looking into…" I gesture at him with a slight flick of my hand.

He stills, leaning back. But at least he finally looks at me and there's a familiar sharpness to the silver-green depths. "If you're here to gloat, get it over with."

I narrow my eyes and Raquel makes some sort of noise behind me. "I'm not here to *gloat*. I'm here to—"

"To what?" His voice holds a dangerous bite. "To help? Run tests? Believe me, *Tara*, there's nothing to do for this."

"Would you just let me look?" I snap.

"Why?" Dejan growls back.

"Because…" Because I don't have a good reason, other than… "I want to."

"Bullshit."

I lurch to my feet. "Fine, what do you want me to say? Yes, I'm unbelievably pissed that you left and destroyed our heartbond. Did you know it left me in the hospital for three days after you did it? I was so *hurt* that I didn't leave the house for almost six months! Fates, what do you want me to say?" I scoff. "That what was left of your 'family' was all over me for months after you disappeared, thinking I knew something about where you were even though I very clearly did not? That my family got wrecked in all the fallout that left me sorting through even more lies from you?"

I'm pacing now, tablet forgotten on the cot. At least he still looks at me.

"And even through all of that, even though I'd have felt so *vindicated* if you came crawling back...I still don't want to see you like this." My voice threatens to break over the admission. I've been trying to deny it, talk around it while researching. But he can still get me to bare at least part of my heart.

Raquel watches wide-eyed. We've worked together for four years, are friends, but she's never heard all this. No one really knows anything about me from before. The young elf who hid behind words and designer clothes and pretended to be content with life until she had her heart broken. The one who finally learned to control her temper and not use it to force people to give her what she wanted. The one who finally left behind an extremely comfortable life in uptown Detroit to pursue a dream of med school and running medical outreach programs like she had always dreamed of doing, and never looked back.

"Tare, I didn't—" It's soft.

"You didn't know?" I snap. "Because you never bothered to look back, did you?"

"No." The gentle agreement almost has me raging again. But I muster myself, take another breath.

"Can I take a look? Please?"

Dejan holds my stare for so long that I think he's checking out again. But he just nods. "What do you need?"

A huff breaks from me. "A lot of things, but mostly just to do some scans for now. I obviously couldn't get ahold of your medical records for just 'professional curiosity.'"

"They'd have probably handed them over if you'd said you were planning to murder me."

I give a double take at the slightest hint of wry humor and catch the faintest spark in his eye. And, Fates help me, a slight smile twitches the corner of my mouth. "Pissing people off wherever you go?"

The wryness spreads up to an arch of his eyebrows and another quirk at the mouth. "I haven't changed all that much."

That almost makes it all worse. Because from the few minutes I've spent around him, and not just trying to stare daggers into him, I can tell that he *has* changed and it's for the better. He trusts people and they trust him. And it feels like he's found purpose with the Drax Guard, like I finally found in medicine.

But I'm not going to offer anything about myself. Because if I can't figure this out and he leaves? It might already be hard enough to actually watch him walk away this time.

"This way." I gesture towards the other side of the building where most of the imaging equipment is. Raquel jostles my shoulder as we head over there and shoots me a raised brow and, okay, a pretty judgmental look. I steadfastly ignore it, keeping one eye over my shoulder to make sure that Dejan follows.

He makes it over, still cognitively with us as far as I can tell. His hands are in pockets and his stance is guarded, bracing, and ready to fight. The number of times I'd seen that exact pose...

But without the hat. That one is still throwing me. So is the slightly unruly hair. It used to always be neatly styled to match the designer clothes he'd wear. Baseball caps would have been nowhere near past De'janick's wardrobe.

I'm staring, and probably about to get punched by Raquel.

"Okay, stand behind the screen. Hat off as well as armor and anything else metal."

He seems almost more offended that he's got to take the hat off. I'm going to have Raquel put the electrodes on for the full heart scan. I'm not going anywhere near shirtless Dejan. I'm not that stupid.

He tosses the hat off and grabs the chain at his neck, pulling out ident tags, about to draw them over his head when a thudding rocks the buildings and shouts echo. Dejan's hat is back on and he rushes past me, but the door flings open before he gets there.

Remy and one of the dragonwalkers are in first, supporting each other. Blood coats the side of Remy's face and Iosef has an arm tucked up to his chest.

"Help Athina!" Remy jerks his head back to the door, waving off Dejan as he makes for them. I turn to Raquel, but she's already moving, helping the two to empty cots, grabbing the radio clipped to the back of her belt and calling for backup.

Cieran is through next, half-carrying Athina. Her arm is around his neck and she's wavering. The blood coating her leg hiked up from the ground is why. He's part terrified, part angry, and I know he's trying to control the heartbond between them. She is too, the way her hand clutches at his arm wrapped around her torso. They're sending signals to each other, trying to keep the other calm.

It almost breaks my heart.

"This way!" I slide my arm around her, helping them over to the other surgical bed beside Dimos, who's pushed up on one elbow like he's about to jump up and help.

"Anyone else severely hurt?"

"One of the kids," Cieran grunts as he gets Athina onto the bed. "Bes and Takis have the three we grabbed."

"Raquel!" I shout. "Who's on the way?"

"Angie and Drew!"

"We've got injured kids as well."

"Okay." She grabs the radio again, her other hand keeping a gauze pad pressed to the side of Remy's head.

We get Athina lying down, her coppery skin already paling. I scrub in, not bothering with a cover. It's the same slashes across her thigh that I'd stitched up on Dimos. Cieran's beside her, one hand clenched around hers. Athina's head tilts toward him on the thin pillow.

"I got you." His murmur catches my ear.

I cut open the shredded trousers, peeling them away from the injury site. Some threads cling to the slashes. I've got bits cleared before I realize that it's just me and I need an extra pair of hands to help. I glance over my shoulder, but the nursing team rushes around, getting everyone taken care of. Then a quiet voice breaks through.

"Pain meds. Hang tight."

I whirl around, and it's Dejan. His gloved hands slide a needle into the crook of Athina's arm. Cieran relaxes, probably due to the fact that Athina has now.

"Dampener?" Dejan asks.

Cieran scowls back.

Dejan huffs. "Just don't be stupid."

Then he stands across from me, handling the irrigator. I just stare for a second before that familiar challenging look spears across his face and I shift back to motion. He knows what he's doing, knowing what I need before I do.

"I'm the team medic." He answers my unspoken question as he hands me some forceps clamped around gauze.

"Since when?" I can't help the question as I use it to clear blood and hand it back. He'd supposedly been about to start studying finance at Vinland University across the A.S.A. border like me before he'd vanished. That was probably just another lie.

He dumps the gauze in a bowl and preps the forceps with clean material. "Since someone I used to know dreamed about being a doctor."

I can't look at him, afraid to parse through the quiet words and the way my vision blurs for a second before I blink hard and focus back on the injury in front of me.

I work in silence, routinely checking on Athina. Cieran keeps one eye on her and one on us. Actually, just on Dejan. But I think it's more to make sure he doesn't blank out while in the middle of surgery.

But he doesn't, at least that I can tell. I get to a part where I can't quite get a needle in, so I look to him. He's got magic and if he's the medic, he can get a quick repair in. "Can you—?"

He shakes his head. "I can't call my magic since all this." It's a quiet confession, complete with a glance at Cieran. "Switch with me."

I wordlessly obey, and his gloved hands slide in to take the needle and hold the wound open so I'm free to get a more accurate target. There's some grit and something else in there, so I grab tweezers and fish it out to a grunt and flinch from Athina.

We trade back and continue to work in silence. I almost hate how easy it is to work with him. We finish cleaning and stitching the gouges. I pass my hands over, easing some healing magic in. I'll give another two treatments with magic before taking the stitches out in about eight hours, and she'll be good to go.

They got back much faster this time, and she was in a lot better shape than Dimos.

"Tara!" Raquel rushes over. "One of the kids has got some sort of magic on him, and Reg can't figure it out."

I pull off the gloves, washing hands again before I'm on my way. This time leaving Dejan behind without a glance.

10

DEJAN

TARA IS GONE AND I'm left to clean up. Athina restlessly sleeps, and Cieran still has hold of her hand, but he's tracking everyone else in the building. Remy, now with bandage on his temple, crouches by one of the kids. The small smile on his face as he chats with a little girl clutching a battered teddy bear helps her relax. And reassures me.

He thinks he's not a great dad, but he's amazing with kids. Everyone else seems to be okay, and Tara helps with the last rescued child. I move to the sink to doff my gloves and wash up.

I'd been jamming my lower leg against a rough edge of the bed to try to stay in my own head, but the more time I spent working with Tara, the less pressure I needed. Until all I was doing was standing there and working.

It's not her. It can't be her.

Because the heartbond isn't there, and the curse definitely still is.

"Heartbond" is a bit of a misnomer. It's a connection between two people, linking them, drawing them inevitably together. It's not actually attached to the organ, but to something about the person. Maybe the soul. Ancient peoples called it a heartbond because it's felt in the chest like a cord, pulling and pulling until the two choose each other, cementing it in place. But there's something solid enough about it. Enough for the sorcerer I hired to grab hold of with his magic and cut it in half, digging it out of my chest and cutting my connection with Tara.

Choosing is the big part. The point of no return. And sometimes I think that I didn't really, truly, choose her. Because if I had, maybe I wouldn't have gone through with cutting it out.

"Dej."

I pause, hands still soapy and millimeters from the water. Cieran stands beside me. He's calmer. A lot calmer.

"I'm sorry," he says.

I shake my head. "You're right to be angry at me." I gather the will to look at him. He's got the thoughtful look on but at least he's not spitting mad. "I would have been the one to cost a life if it came down to it. Not you."

"I should have seen you were off. I don't think I wanted to."

"I didn't want you to." I dip my hands under the still-running water and scrub. "But I should have said something. I just…"

He nudges my shoulder. "Hey, lost you for a second."

I curse softly. Water still runs and my hands are completely clean. "How long?"

"Not long. You just sort of trailed off."

But snapped back quicker than the last few times. At least I remember what I was trying to say.

"I spent the first part of my life not really caring what got left in my wake. Until I met Tara. But I ended up abandoning her. I walked away from Detroit without much thought or care of what I was leaving behind. I didn't want to make the same mistake again. Not in the place I feel like I really belong."

"I get it," Cir says softly.

I don't think he really does. Not completely anyway.

"We'll figure this out, Dej."

The same scoff builds in my chest, trying to hammer at the stone forming there. Drying my hands, I turn to lean against the sink. "I've looked high and low. There's no cure."

"So talk to me. What's it doing to you?"

He still wants answers, wants facts and data and ways he can try to plan around this. What I really need is for him to plan for after I'm gone. "It's leaching away at my emotions, thoughts, magic...I think it's literally calcifying my heart somehow."

He scrapes a hand across his jaw and curses.

"Yeah." I check to make sure Remy is as far away as he can be, out of hearing. "Best I can figure is she meant to make him completely docile. If you can't think or feel or realize what's happening, just blindly obey whatever anyone tells you..." I can't manage to finish the thought.

Cieran looks just as sick as I feel. And, once again, I have no regret about stopping this from happening to Remy. If that fae wasn't dead already, I'd be hunting her down with the last shreds of humanity I have left and making sure she couldn't touch him or Bear ever again.

"How is she?" I tilt my chin to Athina, needing to change the subject.

He rests a hand just beside her head. She turns toward him, eyes flickering and lips moving a moment before she settles back. "She's okay. Thanks for helping."

My arms jam across my chest, and I nod. I still am not sure how I managed to keep present for that long.

"You seemed more like *you* when you were working." Cieran doesn't seem to have any problem noticing the same thing I did.

I shrug, not about to pin the blame, or success, on Tara. She doesn't need me around, no matter how much she "wants to help."

And I don't want her pity.

"You cut your heartbond with her." The quiet statement leaves no room for any answer but the truth.

My arms press tighter across my chest. "Young, stupid, desperate to get away, thinking I was maybe protecting her. I don't have a good reason other than I was selfish and trying to escape some shit and didn't care enough to ask her to come with me."

Almost against my will, I find her across the room. She sits next to one of the kids, and a smile—a real smile—spreads across her face as they talk. She never used to bring that smile out for anyone other than me. It was always something that felt more guarded. It's good to see her like this, even if that smile's going to fade the next time she looks at me.

"You should probably tell her all that." Cieran moves again, still able to keep an eye on me and the room and take Athina's hand into his. She sighs again, and this time the pang that needles me every time I see them together since the Wastelands doesn't come.

"Hey." He nudges me again and it's clear I drifted off again.

I manage a smile. "Doubt I can stay mentally present long enough to get it all out."

"I'll stick around and punch you whenever you blank out." His normal smirk shines through the fatigue and worry.

"I think she can handle that one all by herself."

"Mm...shh." Athina's face twists and she tugs on Cieran's hand. This time the fond look he turns to her does sting a little. And it's not just because Tara is coming back over, face set like it used to when she was ready to argue and get her way.

"You ready to get back to it?" she asks.

Before I can say no, or not to worry about it, Cieran alerts. "To what?"

Tara's cheeks redden slightly then fade, and I'm starting to stare at her. The same passion and energy is still there, just refined into something healthy and good. Helping her work earlier had brought a faint bit of bittersweet happiness for her. She went and did what she'd dreamed about and became a damn good doctor. I jerk my gaze away, focusing on something else across the room.

"Right before you all came in, I'd asked...Dejan...if I could do some tests to maybe help with the..." She gestures at my chest.

And I'm staring again. Even with everything swirling between us, she's still going to try because she deeply *cares* about helping people. I'm suddenly a little glad the stoneheart's in place because otherwise I might have done something stupid like fall for her again.

"He said there's no cure."

Guess I should be grateful that Cieran believes me over a doctor. I could have been lying to him for all he knows.

"Yeah, that's basically what all the research and some colleagues told me when I asked earlier."

A little jolt runs through me. "You did?"

Her face flushes again and a quick look at me doesn't hold as much venom as it did earlier. "I said I wanted to help, so I'm going to see if there's anything I can do." Back to Cieran. "I'd been prepping to run some tests and scans when you all came in."

"You think you could find something?" Cieran apparently doesn't believe me that much since he's already got that look about him—ready to plunge headfirst into whatever stupid scheme might have a chance of working. That's a big reason I like him and was okay with him taking over as sergeant almost nine months ago. The other reason? He doesn't bullshit and he looks after his people no matter what. I could learn a few lessons from him.

Tara shrugs, her hands finding their way into her coat pockets. Bits of blood are splattered across the white from where she'd leaned against the table while working on Athina.

"I don't know. I don't have fancy equipment out here. This is just a field hospital, but...can't really hurt to try, right?"

Cieran nods before she finishes, and I roll my eyes slightly.

"I get a say in this?" I ask.

"Yes, but also no." Cieran's got half a "sergeant" look on. The other half is relief that someone else can look. Between Tara's determined expression and Cieran's optimism, I can't bear to tell them that whatever she'll find will just be bad.

11

Tara

The room is quieting down, and Dejan's sergeant doesn't give him much more of a chance to argue. Dejan just sighs, looking like his old self for a moment, before starting to lay aside the weapons belts and unstrapping the vest. He pauses, fingers faltering on his archer brace before Cieran nudges him and he jolts.

Boots thud, and I tilt a look over my shoulder. The other two crewmembers come over, questions in their faces.

"Doc's going to run a few tests," Cieran supplies and Dejan's face crinkles into a scowl.

"Think you'll find anything?" Besim asks. I'd finally gotten his name as he helped keep kids calm a few minutes ago. I spent three seconds around him and have been trying to figure out how the man stays so patient with Dejan around.

"Probably not," Dejan mutters and O'Donnell kicks his ankle. I wave Raquel over as Dejan shrugs out of the chain mail, showing off his built physique plenty well under the thermal.

Yeah, I'm not going near him when he takes the shirt off.

"You're up," I mutter to Raquel, and she looks proud of me for maintaining some distance. I turn on the scanners and make sure they're all feeding to my tablet.

Raquel has him lie down and starts putting electrodes across his chest. Waves start bouncing up and down on the screen, but...

I frown, making sure it's not feeding in upside down or something.

"EKGs don't look like that, right?" Remy asks, brow pinching as he stares at the tablet.

"Not usually." I hand the device to Raquel, curiosity moving me over to Dejan and feeling for a pulse at the wrist. It's there. Faint, but there. But like the EKG, his pulse bounces all over the place, like his heart is working extra hard to push blood through. The waves aren't following any pattern at all. I've never seen anything like this, even on patients with severe heart failure, past the point of any magic-aided intervention.

I pull a scanner over, holding it above his sternum, and watch the readout. His heart is struggling, but he's not showing any physical signs of it. No shortness of breath or labored breathing, no hypoxemia, no coughing.

My frown is going to take over my whole face. I push the scanner back over to the wall and cue up my magic. It coats my hand in a silver-green sheen and I reach to touch his chest.

He jolts, eyes wide and locked on to my hand at the same exact moment my wrist is pinned in an iron grip. The warlock holds me, the same sort of wild-eyed panic as in Dejan's face. A warning buzz of energy pulses through his grip.

"Remy." Cieran's quiet voice breaks in.

Remy drops my hand and mutters a "sorry," before turning away. Dejan grabs his arm, something wordless passing between them before Dejan releases and Remy steps away, a shuddering breath pulling from him.

I tuck my arm back towards my chest, not hurt, but reeling a bit from what just happened. Raquel is poised on her feet, ready for whatever I need. Which is to avoid some sort of confrontation next to my expensive equipment.

"Sorry. Go ahead." Dejan pulls my attention back to him. He's still tensed up, and I can feel the same radiating from Remy behind me.

"Would it help to sit up?" I ask.

He swings his feet over the edge before I can blink. "Go ahead."

But I still look at his crew, getting the all-clear from O'Donnell before bringing my magic back. I hesitate a moment, perhaps waiting to be grabbed again. Nothing happens, so I gingerly press my hand to his chest.

He's not looking at me, and it gives me the space to focus. His heart is working, struggling, against *something* coating it. I push a little harder. His medical records would have the results of a scan like this, but feeling it in person?

His heart is covered in a sheen of stone, and I can feel the binding spells wrapping around it, squeezing, trying to worm further into that nebulous place where the will resides. There's no physical place for it, the soul. The great debate between scholars and religious. But maybe this fae caster figured out a way to tap into it, because I can almost feel the spell-stone reaching out into something.

I also feel something else. Something interesting. I keep my hand in place and turn slightly, bringing Remy into view. "Can you come back over here?"

A quizzical look is all I get. I tilt my head, urging him to cautiously come back over. "Can I feel your magic again?"

Some panic flares around him. "I didn't hurt you, did I?"

"No." I hold out my free hand. "But I think you inadvertently helped me find something."

Remy rests his hand over mine and I get that same wild-tinted pulse again. Something almost burning and bitter wells in the back of my mind. Fire magic. Strong too. I keep hold of that sensation and focus back in on my scan.

Same thing.

I pull away, killing the connection. Dejan pulls in a deeper breath and his eyes glint a little brighter. This close, and *not staring* at them, it's like I hadn't noticed that they'd been...dull. And I get the tang of his magic. Just for an instant, but from the way he's looking at his hands, he felt it too.

"Well?" Remy's anxious question pulls me back.

"Can I ask what exactly happened? I know that might be a sensitive topic in a lot of different ways, but..."

O'Donnell gestures to Remy and Dejan. They don't look thrilled to relay it.

"We were tracking a fae," Remy starts. There's a lot to this story. A whole lot from the way his shoulders curl in, almost nausea creasing around his eyes. "She had me pinned, was going to hit me with some spell. All I remember was silver on her hand." I get another apologetic look. "Then Dej tackled her off me and she cast it on him instead. After...after she was taken care of, he wasn't moving."

A twinge that I shouldn't be feeling hits. What would have happened if I'd heard that he'd died? Not cared with a void of fifteen years between us?

"Then this idiot just hit me with three bursts of raw magic," Dejan says.

"I didn't know what else to do. You *weren't moving.*"

"I taught you three different healing spells." Dejan rolls his eyes.

"Yeah, not for 'this stupid elf just got hit with some mystery spell so guess I'll let him nap it off.'"

O'Donnell looks ready to jump in and referee if needed, but Besim just looks like they finally need to talk it out.

"It *firren* hurt, Rem."

"Serves you right for getting in her way."

"Oh, I'm *so* sorry for trying to save your life."

Do I need to back away? From the slight edge to their words, maybe they do need to have this out. As long as Dejan doesn't just blank out again. But there's a fresh alertness around him that hasn't been there for the last eight hours.

"I'm about to hit you again."

"Would it make you feel better?" This comes sardonic and familiar.

"*Fir* you." But there's some relief to Remy's voice and he gently taps a fist to Dejan's shoulder. They both nod, and that seems settled.

I don't get it.

"Thoughts, Doc?" comes O'Donnell's somewhat wry question.

I shift, refocusing and giving up trying to figure out these two guys. "I picked up some other traces of magic in there, and it's his." I point to Remy.

"Is that good or bad?" He pulls back again, arms crossed and palms pressed to his sides. Dejan looks ready to punch him for some other reason entirely than the words they'd just traded.

"Good." I pause again, really wishing I knew what had and hadn't already been established by his doctors. But I think I'm putting some stuff together.

"This is my theory." Fates, I also wish I had more background on the mission because I don't want to freak Remy out again or bring something else back for him. "You used your magic right after the fae spellcasting and it brought him back?"

Remy nods. Dejan watches me and I try not to focus solely on him.

"Most of what I read on 'stoneheart' was pretty theoretical or 'this hasn't been used in a thousand years', so I'm spitballing a little here."

They don't seem to care.

"But from what the research says, I think maybe she was...'taken care of' before she finished casting it. I don't know if that's a good thing or not."

"Sounds real convincing," Dejan says. I arch an eyebrow and he silences.

"It's a..." Another glance at Remy. "A pretty significant compulsion spell."

Remy looks at his feet. Dejan lightly kicks his leg and Cieran nudges the warlock's shoulder.

"Um, but from what you described, either she didn't finish it or her power getting cut off right after didn't give it a chance to seal off. It's continuing to grow without direction. Remy putting raw magic in immediately after kept it from just putting Dejan in a coma and dying. I think that's the only reason you came back and have been able to function this long." I finally turn to Dejan.

From what little I gleaned in researching, he probably shouldn't have woken back up after the fae was killed.

"Function seems like a strong word." *There's* the undercurrent of bitterness I remember.

"You have better moments," I say and almost regret it because that admits that I've been keeping at least one eye on him.

"Physical contact helps." He darts a look at his team. "Ironic, I know."

Small smiles are passed around. So he hasn't really changed that way. But this is the most I've seen him talk and engage, so something has happened.

"It's better around Rem."

"We holding hands from now on?" Remy asks, lips twitching. Dejan shoots back something in elvish that has my ears burning but O'Donnell laughing. It breaks a smile from Remy. He probably understood it.

"Do I just point out that this is the best he's been in a while?" Besim cuts in, a faint smile on his face, but there's some uncomfortable knowing there. Dejan scowls at him, and my face definitely heats a few degrees or twenty.

"Anyone else put that together about Rem's magic?" Cieran asks and Dejan shakes his head.

"They might have just assumed it was part of the spell."

"Probably also because Remy wasn't in the room for them to catch his magic," I put in.

"So where do we go from here?" Cieran hooks his hands into his tac vest collar.

"I'm not sure," I admit and hate doing so. I'd been excited to find the thread of Remy's magic still helping Dejan hold on to awareness, but don't know if there *is* a next step. "The spell is still wound really tight. I don't know what actually gets rid of it besides the original caster. That's all the research had and that's probably what you've been told already."

Dejan nods, jaw setting in an expression I once knew. He tugs the electrodes off and pulls his shirt back on.

"I'll put in for discharge when we get back. Agents will be here soon, right?" he asks the sergeant. Cieran nods, all levity gone.

Dejan gathers up his gear, armored vest hanging from one hand. "Thanks for trying," he tells me and strides off. The door clacks shut behind him and it feels almost *final.*

"Rem," the half-troll says quietly. I haul my gaze back to the three soldiers still standing around me.

"I *know*!" Remy's voice rises, and so does the heat around us with a warning beep from the machines. He sucks in a breath and everything quiets, including him. "I know." Misery lines his face as he crosses his arms, and presses palms flat against his sides. "What am I supposed to do?"

Besim just gives a tight smile. "Stop blaming yourself."

Remy shakes his head until Cieran grabs his shoulder. "She'd have had to kill every single one of us before we let that happen to you, Rem."

I don't want to fill in the pieces.

"He saved your life," I say softly. It's almost a question, like I hadn't just heard what Dejan had done to save his teammate.

Remy nods, barely meeting my gaze. "He's one up on me now." His words come thick. "And now he's what? Just going to fade out?" The warlock's look sears through me, and then the others like they can do anything else about it.

My chest tightens as I realize that he's just giving voice to the same turmoil raging in their eyes. They really care about Dejan.

"Maybe with what we just discovered, the specialists back in Dunhare can figure something out." It's paltry. I haven't had to give bad news in awhile, not since leaving the main hospital in Seattle to start this program. I might be out of practice.

"We'll figure something out, Rem." Cieran's reassurance is steadier. "Go get some rest."

The warlock looks a beat from refusing, and a new look falls over Cieran. I'm suddenly fighting the urge to stand taller and start saluting.

Remy glares a little, then gives in. "Fine. But if he's not back in fifteen minutes, I'm gonna go find him."

"Okay," Cieran easily agrees, and nudges his soldier toward the cots. Besim flashes a faint smile at me that feels like a thank you.

"Is *he* going to be okay?" I point after Remy.

Cieran hesitates a moment. "Losing a brother is never easy," he says. "Thanks for trying, Doc."

They follow Remy and I'm left staring after them. *Brother.* I'm an only child, but seeing the way Dejan interacted with them is a little like how Raquel and her siblings interact. There's stories behind their words— *"He's one up on me now."* It's not the first time they've saved each other's lives. *"I wasn't going to let that happen."* Dejan's words earlier had held a promise that he'd do it again and again to save Remy. Probably Besim and Cieran too.

Everything from him helping me with Athina, to seeing his magic come back for a moment, and finally admitting how much he's changed...it's muddling the anger and leaving confusion in its wake. Remy might go find Dejan in fifteen minutes, but I'm going to go sooner. The two of us might need to truly talk.

12

DEJAN

"DEJAN?" TARA'S QUIET VOICE brings me back.

I got outside and halfway through arming back up before I blanked out again. That moment of feeling like myself didn't last as long as everyone thought it might.

"Hi," I reply, still not looking at her. Going to the sheltered bench between the buildings had seemed easiest for someone to find me in case I clocked out. I'd been right. I snug the straps of the vest into place and slide my archer's brace on, trying not to think how this might be the last time I ever do it. Two-hundred-year life expectancy. Didn't think forty-five was going to be where I tapped out.

"You're back?"

"For now." A sharp and brittle sound escapes with my words.

"You okay?" she asks.

"Pretty sure we all know the answer to that." I finally look at her before sliding knives into place. I wish the action made me feel comfortable like it normally does, but there's just that same nothing.

"Dejan." She's still got a quietness to her voice.

"What do you want, Tara?" I snap, wanting her there and wanting her gone all at once.

She sighs, frustrated. "Can we talk?"

I want to say no, but I owe her something for trying. And a whole lot more for leaving fifteen years ago. So I set my sword against the bench and gesture to the empty spot.

Tara takes it, a gap between us.

"I'm really sorry," she starts. "About what happened to you. I still am pissed, by the way. Maybe wished something would happen to you, but..."

"So partial maiming would have been okay?"

The look she tilts at me has me faintly smiling and a sensation tries to spread in my chest. Tries, and gets quashed instantly.

"We both know why I was better for a few minutes in there," I say. Because her magic had been poking around and some part of my heart still remembers it, remembers her.

"Yeah." She looks at her hands, fingers gripping each other like she regrets it.

"Tara." Fates, starting this off is worse than going into a fight with odds stacked against me. "You knew I wasn't into good stuff when we met."

She stills, maybe ready, maybe not, to actually hear this. But I do know that I don't have much time, and I need to get this out while I still can.

"My father ran the biggest drug ring along the Allied States and Vinland border. The Kostic Shrike clan. He didn't really want me to be 'part' of it, sort of giving the illusion to anyone watching that I wasn't tied up in it all. But—" My palms scrape each other. "I was a dealer. I was learning the ins and outs of the business to take over one day. I just did it, mostly because I didn't have anything else to do, or anywhere else to go. Mom had vanished when I was fourteen. My cousin is still past head deep in it all. I wasn't close to anyone, and everyone I knew was in the clan."

She barely moves, still not really looking at me, just like I'm not quite making eye contact with her.

"Then I met you. I was making a delivery on campus that day."

Caught sight of her, and when she'd looked back, the heartbond had activated. It had been the best and worst day of my life. Because after years of feeling isolated, suddenly I wasn't alone. And it almost physically hurt.

"I told you a lot of lies because I didn't want to ruin the life you had. It looked pretty great."

A show she put on, like I'd put one on for her.

Tara finally moves. "Guess we both lied to each other."

"Yeah." My reply comes a little sad. "My dad, when he found out, wanted to leverage our heartbond to get in with your parents. Why bother with cash when you have a top banker and financier in your pocket?"

I'd been there for some of the meetings. From her sharp inhale, she'd found out the hard way that her father had been setting up accounts and managing a shell game to keep clan money moving and distracting the Feds. He'd gotten some time too, but high-tier financiers never stayed long behind bars.

"Once I figured out the heartbond and how to stop some things from getting through to you, I just got more restless. Hell, you remember what I was like."

She nods, still silent. We were kids. Barely thirty—the equivalent of human nineteen-year-olds. I'd been arrogant, sharp-tongued, reckless. Things that have been tempered a little in the intervening years. Had to be after over a year of living on the streets to further scramble my trail.

"Dad started expanding the business. I was getting roped further and further in. I didn't want that life. Didn't want to have to keep it from you. You always deserved someone better than me." That had always been one of my truths, but now I don't feel anything when I say it.

"Dejan." She shakes her head and my hand flicks between us, silently asking her to let me finish.

"Desperate, angry, horrified at myself—that was me almost every minute. It was going to tear your family apart eventually, everything my dad had yours doing or maybe even just me hanging around. I knew I couldn't just leave, or they'd haul me back, and pull you into everything too. They wouldn't hesitate to hurt you to keep me in line."

I'd known that even before my dad made his first veiled threat. I force a breath. "So I pulled together records, samples, evidence. Took it to the Feds. Traded it all in exchange for amnesty. Turned down the witness protection." *Righteous action burnishes a tarnished name.* That was a centuries-old Kostic saying. But maybe still just an excuse.

"You disappeared," she finishes. Right after I apparently landed her in hospital by getting the heartbond removed in a black-market warehouse by a sorcerer I'd tracked down through some of my dad's contacts. I wasn't doing so great myself either at the time. It felt like my chest had been torn in two and I was missing half of myself.

"I told myself it was to keep you safe, but it was really to keep them from getting to me through you. Cutting off all traces to me. I knew how to disappear. Couldn't have a loose thread."

"I would have come with you." It's accusing, lonely, angry.

I shake my head. "No. It was a year of lying low, avoiding hits put out by my cousin who somehow escaped the arrests and trials that got Dad jail for life. You had a future. I didn't. I never did back then."

"Why didn't you tell me?" She turns to face me, and I have to look at her this time.

She was the first person to really make me laugh. I'd snuck out to see her a few nights after the bond activated and she'd convinced me to run out into a rainstorm with her. And even as we slipped and laughed and felt *free* for one moment, the truth snuck in. I'd never be able to hide her, or the bond, from my father.

And even if she was the only person I dared to trust a little, the one who made me dare to dream of *more*...there was still only the bleak truth.

"Because I was made up of so many different lies and broken dreams, and heartbond or not, you weren't going to want *me*. You've always had a better path away from me."

We just had to look around to see it.

"I didn't get to make that decision." Anger sparks in her eyes. "And you shouldn't have made it for both of us."

"I just...I don't think I loved you the way you thought you loved me, Tara. I just don't. We're better off apart. The Fates messed up when it came to us."

She spins away, arms crossing, shoulders lining up. Probably even more pissed now. She jerks to her feet and faces off with me. "I did love you, Dejan. I really did. You don't think you showed me the real you, but you did. Those nights on the roof, meeting under the willow trees on campus, the winter carnival..."

All memories I've shoved away into a tiny box in the back of my head. Hearing her mention them only brings faint impressions, lacking color and sound and linked emotion.

"And you just..." Her hands fling out between us and fall back to her sides. "I guess I just want to know if any of it meant anything to you. What you said just now...everything you said back then...I thought heartbonds were supposed to be different. I guess I just want to know if this would have happened eventually. We'd grow apart and angry and bitter and have it cut out anyway."

She sniffs and wipes at her eyes, and some forgotten part of me wants to reach out to her, but that's not going to end well.

"We were just an escape for each other, Tara. Neither of us was going to leave or change. We were just going to use each other and chase some...some high. And eventually..." I shrug. Maybe she's right. Eventually this would have happened.

Two years of a heartbond and I'd never made steps to move forward. To elves, heartbonds are as good as married. There's an official "binding" ceremony to make everything legal, but we'd never planned one. And those usually happen within months of a new bond.

I didn't want her around my father or cousin. Didn't want her drawn into their life. Didn't want to live in the compound, pretend to be normal, pretend like she wouldn't be used if I stepped off the line or threatened anyone's position in the clan. Even if we lived somewhere else, I'd always have eyes on me. Would never really be out. Not unless I made sure there wouldn't be anyone around. And I was selfish enough that it didn't include Tara.

Back then, I didn't know what genuine love or relationship was. I had no example or context for it. Didn't really risk myself for anything or anyone. Until I got out, and started meeting people. People like my old paramedic partner who didn't take my bullshit but the way he corrected was gentle and helpful under the sightly acerbic tone. Like Besim's parents who have a rock-solid marriage and almost scared me with how honest and kind and loving they are to everyone. And even in the last year, seeing Cieran and Athina's bond and the way they're working tirelessly to make each other stronger despite the miles between them.

"You should have told me," she says.

"I should have done a lot of things," I softly reply.

"I get the parts about your dad and wanting to leave, and I wish you'd have told me more back then. But everything else about you and me? You said you told a lot of lies. I think you're still telling yourself some."

And she leaves, posture like she's got her arms braced over her stomach, trying to hold everything in until she gets somewhere quiet to let it all out. Once, that would have been on my shoulder. Now it's probably just a quiet corner.

That's one of the few things I was good at back then. Knowing what would stop the tears and bring a smile back to her face, even if sometimes I'd been the one to bring them out in the first place.

I turn back to my hands, scarred from missions. One at the base of my right thumb is from a small explosion in the drug lab. She'd been the best thing to ever happen to me, and I'd walked away from her. We're better off apart, and I hope that somewhere in the words we traded, she finds some closure. Because I'm not going to be around long enough to give her anything else to help her finally move on.

13

Tara

I barely make it to my office before the tears well and truly start to fall. The sobbing comes once the door clicks, and I don't even make it across the room to the cot. Knees tuck up to my chest and arms wrap around them, tugging myself into a ball on the floor and trying to smother every emotion wringing its way out.

And I thought it couldn't hurt worse.

Gasping breaths escape, and shuddering inhales make room for more. Rivers flow down my cheeks, soaking my lips with salty water. Probably mixed with mucus for good measure, because fifteen years are coming out one way or another.

A part of my brain dimly registers how close I am to hyperventilating, and I make myself get up out of the nearly fetal position and give my lungs a chance to expand and make the sobbing worse.

I get to the cot and grab my pillow, strangling it as rage starts to break through, urging me to hurl it across the room. But grief wants to curl around it. And the small part trying to think in all the mess is telling me not to break anything.

I don't think I loved you the way you thought you loved me is going to haunt me forever.

Mom had never liked him. Guess he just proved her right about a lot of things. The sobbing slows, hiccuping every other breath as I sit there, pillow balled up in my lap, and stare hollowly across the room.

Maybe I should be glad there's no heartbond anymore, because feeling him blocking me out on the other end would be making this worse. Feeling him believe it when he said we were better off apart. Not like I hadn't been telling myself that for fifteen years. But I want to know if he really believes it. Because some lonely nights, I miss him and all the good times that exist as gold-tinted memories in my head.

A few lingering tears sneak down my cheeks, splashing on my sleeves. I use the cuff of my coat to wipe my face.

It's almost ten p.m., but I'm not about to go to sleep. No, I need to move around, do something to forget the last few minutes, and put off another round of crying before I start thinking about it all again.

I'm vain enough to use some magic to ease the puffiness around my eyes, shoo some of the redness away. I go through several tissues before ditching the white coat and pulling on a plain long-sleeve shirt. Autumn days are still warm in the desert, but the nights make up for it.

Our camp has long settled down. A distant coyote howls. Moonlight is scarce around cloud cover and a dwindling crescent. I never did get around to dinner. I'm not hungry anymore. But I need to check on the injured dragonwalkers, and probably go check back on the kids. Halfway to the surgical building, I falter. I'm pretty sure the crews are bunking down in or around the building, and I don't know where Dejan went. Hopefully Remy didn't have to go find him staring into space. The last thing I want is to run into Dejan right now, so I alter my path to the smaller dormitory building we set the kids up in.

Some of the refugee women had seen them and had come to help. They'd brought colorful blankets, and helped with baths, or braiding hair. And gave plenty of songs and comforting smiles. The languages were all over the place—common, Slavic and Nordic elvish, Mexican-Iberian. But smiles and kindness span a lot of differences.

One more glance at the main building, and I gently push the dormitory door open. A gentle rustle draws my attention across the darkened room. A shadowy figure leans over one of the beds. The night shift nurse checking on a kid. The lights aren't on, and somehow the nightlight got knocked over.

I go to straighten it when my boot kicks something soft. A faint grunt draws my gaze down. In the dim light, I make out the shape of a crumpled body. It's too big to be a kid, and too awkward for the night shift nurse to be sleeping on the ground. Which means...

Before a gasp can materialize, a hand clamps over my mouth and I'm pulled back against something solid. A low voice hisses, and the figure at the bed mutters back, a faint red glow illuminating masked features before the light jumps to the child. A faint cry of surprise is cut off, and then the man picks up a limp form and slings it over his shoulder.

I lurch forward and get pulled back, something pricking my lower back.

"Don't move," the voice warns in common.

"There's only the four in here," the second growls as he passes us by with the unconscious child. I try to reach out again, and sharpness digs deeper into my skin.

Scarlet light flares again and I blink against it.

"This is the head doc," the man says, snuffing out the light.

"Good. Tell us where the rest of the kids are."

I get a shake when I don't answer, and the hand doesn't let up over my mouth either. I try to think. The Drax soldiers and dragonwalkers are in the building nearby. Our camp guards are somewhere patrolling. Hopefully. I'd hate to find out now that they take the money and sleep all night when they're supposed to be on duty.

"Guards are taken care of and so are those meddling soldiers. Don't scream, or we'll incinerate the camp." I receive another shake, and it sends my stomach flipping another few rounds. *Taken care of.* What does that mean?

"Point us in the direction of the kids. We just want what's ours."

I narrow my eyes. The flipping skids to a halt and anger takes over to chase the fear. He could be bluffing for all I know. But I'm also hoping that the spec ops crews are more than capable of taking out traffickers in their sleep, so I just nod.

Either way, I need to get out of the building, see where they're taking this kid. See what damage they've done. This is what I get for crying and feeling my feelings in my room instead of staying out and about and busy.

He doesn't appreciate my cooperation, tugging and pulling me backward out of the building. It's not until we're out in the open air, one floodlight flickering weakly, that I realize.

There should have been more than four kids in that room. Either someone changed up the rooming plans while I was taking care of the soldiers, or...I already have help out here.

I let them yank me a few more steps, before grabbing hold of the man's arm and dropping my weight down in a move Raquel taught me. A curse of surprise, and hands lash out, grabbing my shirt before I get more than a step away. But my mouth is free, and I scream.

14

Tara

Chaos erupts. Fire roars from somewhere, racing in a wavering light across the ground, and a bellow answers. A whir sends me flinching and a grunt has me staring in shock at the trafficker slowly crumpling to his knees, kid still over a shoulder, arrow deep in his gut.

I dumbly look the opposite direction, seeing Dejan on one knee, bow raised, the new firelight bathing his face set in grim lines. Another arrow is on the string before I can blink, but the man holding me yanks me back, wrapping an arm around my chest. A knife settles under my chin. It jabs and I freeze, warmth trickling down my neck. Cries go up from somewhere and cut off suddenly.

Remy materializes behind Dejan, sword in one hand and deep blue magic swirling around the other.

"Pull back," the man says, and it takes a moment to realize he's not talking to me. I'm wrenched again, the steel never leaving my throat. Dejan rises to his feet, he and Remy stalking forward.

"I'll slice her open," the man calls. I feel him twisting, checking over his shoulders.

"Boss." A breathless gasp announces three other men running over. I'm angled just enough to see limp forms in their hold. Except for one kicking and struggling.

Light flares, and Athina stalks forward, sword out and bright flames coating her free arm. Rows of red scales slant down her cheekbones—halfway shifting. A shadowed figure is at her back. Cieran.

She barely limps and shouldn't be off the cot. I have a feeling they're both sharing the load of that injured leg.

"One more step and she's dead," the man shouts again. "And then we'll kill the kids. Cut our losses here."

O'Donnell comes further into the light, all feral grace. Takis is a few paces away, sword in hand. I wrench my gaze away from his dripping blade.

"Or you can drop your weapons, and let the doc and the kids go, and maybe we won't incinerate you immediately." Cieran prowls forward another step.

There's blood everywhere and I don't know where to look. The blade prods deeper into my neck and this time a whimper breaks free. The anger is gone, replaced by just pure shock and fear.

I don't know why, but my gaze falls to Dejan. He and Remy are a little closer. But he falters, the bow drooping, one boot stumbling a little. Remy's hand, still magic-coated, drops on his shoulder, and he jerks back to alertness.

"Get us out of here," my captor mutters.

A glowing circle spreads around us. Panic starts to set in. The soldiers still hold their positions. Dejan raises his bow and fires, but the arrow deflects midair. The knife jabs harder into my chin.

Dejan's face sets into something grim. He lowers the bow. His mouth moves and Remy replies. The circle grows brighter, things starting to fade in front of me. Then someone shouts as colors whirl. I see Dejan sprinting, jumping through the blazing barrier just as the world goes black for a terrifying moment.

I'm slammed to the ground, ashy dust puffing up and sending me coughing. Dejan crouches over me. The traffickers drop their kids and shout, waving weapons. And it takes two heartbeats of staring at a clouded night sky to realize.

We're not outside the camp.

We're miles away. Deep in the Wastelands.

15

Dejan

Displaced ash and dirt from the Wastelands rise around us. Tara is behind me, and I've got one sword against four. Not bad odds, but I've also got kids to worry about, Tara, and a curse that could leave me drooling on the ground in the next two seconds.

The traffickers yell, trying to get me to put down my sword, threatening anything that's breathing. Magic flares and soars around us, scaring away the darkness. If these idiots don't stop, they'll summon every *firren* thing that lives in the Wastelands. But I'm not moving.

Tara scrambles behind me, her breaths sobbing. I've barely felt anything in three months, but that same *twinge* had hit again at the sight of her panic and the blood dribbling down her neck.

Remy hadn't even argued when I said I was going after her. Just slipped a tracking coin in my pocket, one that I'm going to need to get to her somehow if I don't make it past this point.

"Dejan?" Her quiet voice almost has me turning.

"Drop it!" the lead trafficker shouts again. One calls up some magic, icy-blue flickering and snaring around his hand. Ice warlock.

I don't have anything to counter with. Even if I had more than a few small offensive spells mixed in with my regenerative-based magic, it vanished after those shocking few seconds where I'd felt it again. Before I'd re-broken Tara's heart.

A gasp tears from Tara and this time I do look, and another curse breaks free. The creature from before prowls forward, long head sinuously weaving back and forth. Tara stills, and the thing's fanged mouth parts in some sort of gruesome smile.

"Tara!" I forget the men, forget what I'm doing, only remembering how that thing had sapped everything from me. I reach to grab her shoulder, break her eye-contact with it. But I get hit and thrown away from her, frigid cold snaring around me and pinning me to the ground.

Idiot.

She's still caught in its gaze, but it settles down, tail curling around its taloned feet, keeping her pinned. I try to move, but the magic tightens. I should be *pissed* but all I feel is mild anger, and that makes the me trapped deep in my head rage even more.

"Get everyone inside before we trigger something out here," the leader says.

The magic slithers down my arms, grabbing my wrists and forcing them together, squeezing my right arm until I release the sword. The spell weighs my arms down, so I can't really move as another man edges forward and starts pulling weapons off.

I don't fight back, can't be bothered. The voice in the back of my head is fainter and fainter, and only another look at Tara keeps a blackout away. The man controlling me sends out another bit of magic, ensnaring her wrists the same way. The leader yells a command and the creature backs off, grumbling deep in its chest at giving up its victim.

Tara lurches with another gasp, struggling to her feet, fighting the magic pinning her wrists, bits of her green magic trying to flicker past.

She stumbles and another burst of blue knocks her over. This does bother me slightly, but I'm still not moving as I'm jerked to my feet by the back of my vest.

The magic-user drags her up, shakes her, and something about her wide-eyed fear and confusion has me shifting slightly.

"Move." I'm shoved forward. Most of the kids are still limp figures slung over shoulders. Except for one. I catch a glimpse of bright silver-green eyes in the light before they shutter closed. The elven owner lets his arms sway a little bit more as he's carried.

It almost makes me smile.

"Dejan?" Tara's soft voice draws my focus to where she stumbles at my side. She's confused that I'm here and honestly, I can't blame her. Not after what I told her before it all went to hell.

"It'll be okay," I manage, my voice one degree up from monotone.

"Shut up." My shoulder receives a strike, and I remember how to give a glare at the man. He doesn't care, continuing to poke and prod us forward. And...the *shilsa* has my sword.

That one sneaks through, and my eyes narrow slightly. They keep us walking, not really bothering with a rear guard, or putting out wards to hide their tracks. Guess they think they're far enough out that nothing can find them.

Even if I didn't have a tracker coin, Remy would find us anyway. All he needs is a sliver of something that belongs to a person, and he can track something or someone across a continent. He's got something small for each of us in his tac vest just in case.

These idiots don't know what's coming for them.

Fifteen minutes later, a ruinous building rises before us. Like everything in the Wastelands, it's a shattered remnant of civilization. Collapsing in on itself under the weight of a past war and the ashy fallout of magic and a super-volcano erupting, creating the thousands of miles of dead zone dividing the Allied States.

We're shoved through the door. The parts of the ceiling that have long ago fallen have boards creating a barrier between sky and dirty floor. Boxes and crates are stacked in corners, there's a table with some flickering screens through another door. This looks like it might have been some sort of police station or city center once upon a time, based on the size and warrens of halls and rooms.

Three men emerge from a back hall, one with an arm covered in bandages. The kids are taken into another room, and Tara gets shoved away from me. She lurches, almost like she wants to pull closer, but then doesn't. They herd her in the direction of the kids, and I'm left standing in front of the leader.

"Have a seat." He gestures to a rickety looking folding chair. It's rusty metal, and probably tetanus waiting to happen. So I don't move. It takes two of them to move me forward and push me into the seat.

"First, tell me about your team, *if* they find us."

I dig fingers into my palm. The white noise is starting to come back. It had been a dull background hum for a precious short time after Tara's evaluation, and then kicked to the corner after Remy gave me a burst of magic.

My head jolts and I blink, looking suddenly in a different direction. Latent stinging breaks across my face, throbbing in my nose.

"Do this the easy way, or I'll give you five minutes with the basilisk out back and you'll be begging to talk."

Basilisk? That thing's not a basilisk. It's some sort of contorted monstrosity.

Another punch snaps my head back, and I slowly raise magic-bound hands to wipe blood away.

"Your. Team." He acts like he's so patient.

"I wouldn't be so sure you're safe here," I say.

He scoffs. "This place is warded and out in the middle of the Wastelands. No one's finding us out here, no matter how good."

"Then nothing to worry about, right?" I manage a little smile. I wish I was in my right mind. I'm sure I'd be ready to punch someone and this guy's looking like a really good target.

He narrows his eyes, pulling back to lean against the table. The screens are glitching every few seconds. Either it's the warding, or more likely, the reception just sucks out in the Wastelands. Magic and electronics don't mix and all the magic-gone-wrong out here makes it near impossible to get electronics to work correctly. Unless they're sporting military gear somewhere, they're not going to get a clear signal. Maybe another point in my favor.

Someone grabs my hair, yanking my head back. Another human pins my shoulders, keeping me from moving as the head idiot comes over and pulls out my ident tags.

"Well, look at that. *Kostic*."

That registers among the humming. I'm released, but stay slouched in the chair, barely bothered by the sprawling position.

He pulls out a phone. "Looks like he is."

"What?" I ask.

He gives a sickening sort of smile. "You've got a cousin?"

I just look back. This is bad. Maybe I'm a little glad I can't feel anything, because bringing up Damir is not going to lead anywhere good.

He flips the phone around and I'm treated to a flash of something like a wanted poster. Damir is finally trying to find me and he's willing to pay out to get me alive.

Great.

"So what's your cousin want with you?" he asks.

I know perfectly well what my cousin wants, and it's nothing less than my head on a stake. Probably to send in a box to my dad in prison.

I shrug.

He keeps studying me, maybe trying to figure out if I'm really worth that price tag and if he can negotiate higher. He's going to be disappointed. I haven't kept up with my family at all, but odds are good Damir hasn't turned from his drug-fueled crazy and heavy-handed gang enforcer ways. Probably only to get worse, since he took Dad's place at the head of the Kostic clan.

"He's the snitch?" one of the men asks, grabbing my tags and looking at them again before dropping them to thump against my tac vest they haven't taken yet.

I'm going to have permanent grooves in my hand by the time I die. "The term is 'confidential informant.'"

No one appreciates how hard that was to get out. Instead, I get another punch.

"You screwed up a lot of things up in Detroit."

"Wasn't hard." I spit out some blood. The city runs on illegal.

"So what, you're playing soldier now? I heard you never killed anyone back then, but an A.S.A. uniform makes it okay?" The lead guy scoffs.

I don't answer. Even if I'd trained with knives and bow since I was a kid, the difference is that I would have been killing innocent people fifteen years ago. Now I'm helping clean the earth of people like my cousin and these men. That's a hell of a difference and that twinge hits again. Regret that I can't keep doing it. Probably won't be much help when my team gets here. Can't help Tara and the kids get out.

"Didn't do witness protection or change your name. Guess I can respect you for that," he admits.

Live boldly. That had been a motto of my father. Part of me is still a Kostic, and I'm going to show the world that at least one of us can do something good with our magic.

He pulls out his phone and taps at the screen. I don't know how long I have before I'm face-to-face with my imminent demise. Though I'm willing to bet I've got some time. Damir has always been the kind who didn't mind getting his hands dirty. If he wants revenge, he's coming for me himself.

"This is Baz Linten. I need to talk to Kostic." He turns slightly away. The room seems poised, waiting in the silence that's the person on the other end getting Damir. Or maybe it's just me, trying to figure out my plan as the white noise rushes louder in my ears.

"Kostic." Linten turns back to me. "I've got something you've been looking for."

A pause, then he gives an unpleasant smile, and turns the phone. He snaps a picture of me and sends it, before returning the phone to his ear. "Proof enough?"

Panic, fear? Something is there, but I'm just sitting. Waiting, listening.

"Wire half before you get here. I'll send coordinates. We'll take—"

16

Cieran

Remy beats me to the circle of burned earth. He's already crouched on its outskirts, sifting through the charred earth, palming some crystallized fragments of the transfer gate spell. From what he's said before, there's a limited amount of time to trace a location off a gate circle like this. Depending on how skilled the caster is, and what they leave behind.

I heard part of his and Dej's conversation through comms, but, "Talk to me."

"He's got a tracker coin at least. If they find it, or jump again—" he lifts up his handful of dirt—"I can still track him knowing that he's got some of my magic."

"And if they kill him on sight?" I ask grimly.

"He's going to try to get the coin to Novak." But he doesn't have any more hope for that happening than I do in the very real possibility that Dejan's already dead.

"Shit."

"Yeah." But undeterred, Remy pulls some of his magic, working it into a tracking spell that never misses.

"How was he?" I ask quietly. "Before he jumped."

"He'd started to check out, but I gave him a pulse." Rem holds up his fingers, the same flickering blue as the hottest part of a flame swirling around them. "Seemed more like himself."

And there's hope in his face. I don't want to crush it, not after watching Remy for the last three months and hating the guilt eating away at him. I don't want to lose Dejan, and it's good to know that Remy kicking some more magic around can bring him back. But that's not a viable long-term solution, and we all know it.

"Cir?" Athina limps up. Her mouth purses at the corner, trying to hide how much pain she's in. We don't have the dampeners on, but we've come a long way in reading each other and sharing through the heartbond since meeting almost a year ago.

"Rem's gonna get a direction for us."

"I can't track and do a portal at the same time," Remy says, still crouched. "Not unless you want to bring a blanket and just tuck me in to sleep wherever we end up."

He looks more like himself in this moment, and I tip a grin. "All right, we'll see what we can do."

"We'll take you." Takis steps closer. It's incredibly rude to ask for a ride from shifters in their animal form. But it's a different story if they offer. Even if the fleet's helped us out before, I still wasn't going to assume.

I nod, casting a glance at Athina, but she's already got her brow arched, her "I'm *not* staying behind" crystal clear in the expression. Her affirmation follows loud through our mindspeak.

"I know." I nudge her arm with mine. "You need another dose of something before we go."

"I will locate that nurse." She limps off.

"Cir." Besim strides over, hauling a form by the collar. "Camp guards are all down. One dead and the rest in various states of unconsciousness. This one got stuck."

He tosses the man down, and I recognize his features from the last attack on the trafficker's camp. A cold that comes a little too easily sweeps over me as I look down at the man. It'd be easier to just kill him instead of finding some place to stash him until the agents and some more soldiers show up as backup.

Besim doesn't try to argue one way or another. But he'd prefer to make sure this guy will eventually wake up with a killer headache.

"Where's Tara?" Raquel's voice is part scream, part begging. Takis gets an arm out to catch her before she tackles Remy for answers.

"Easy," Takis murmurs. The nurse turns a shocked look at me.

"You in charge if she's not here?" I ask.

She nods dumbly, lips parting again to ask, but I hold up a hand. "I need you to keep everything running, get ready for the Bureau team that's coming in. We'll get the camp soldiers over to the med building before we take off. We're on rescue and recover." I smile, but it doesn't reassure her.

"They have her?" she asks quietly.

"Yeah. But Remy's already on it. He's the best tracker in the entire Guard. We'll get everyone back home."

"Okay." She rubs at her arms, a tear snaking free, before she musters a breath.

"You with me?" I ask.

She nods, drawing in another breath. "Yeah. Um. What about when the agents get here?"

"We'll find out." Besim jerks his chin to the entry gate. Headlights announce three trucks pulling up.

"Takis, you and Bes go let them in."

The dragonwalker tips a nod and he and Besim jog off. The man Bes dumped is stirring. I'm not going to *take care of him* in front of the nurse, but I clip his head with my boot, sending him right back to sleep. She makes some sort of noise in protest. I don't have any sympathy for him. She can if she wants.

"Got it." Remy rises from the ground, brushing his hands off. "Wastelands." There's apology in the words, and an immediate check-in from Athina through the bond at the way my gut still knots at the word, two full years later.

"Sweet," I say. *Where's Iosef?* I ask through the mindspeak.

Getting the children settled. He'll meet us at the gate.

Iosef was the reason we had any realization they were in the compound. He'd gone to check on the dragonwalker kids, getting some gut feeling that everything wasn't okay, and ran into a trafficker who won't be getting back up. He sent an alert through the mindspeak to his team, who then passed it to us. He stayed put, keeping a cloaking spell over most of the kids, but apparently hadn't gotten them all.

You okay? I ask.

I will be fine.

She's sounded more convincing, but we've got things to do, and she's not going to be left behind. We need all hands on deck, and I'm a hell of a lot more comfortable taking Athina, even wounded, than I am a stranger.

You are so sweet sometimes.

Get out of my head.

She just laughs, and seconds later limps back out.

The trucks pull up to where we still stand. Besim and Takis hop off the sides where they hitched a ride back over. Agency guards step out, and one with captain stripes comes over. I try not to grimace. He's very aware of his importance.

A silver-haired woman is out next, power practically rippling off her. Like all fae, she looks ageless, and her pointed ears and angular features have a sort of luminous appearance. She wears her short hair spiked, and an Agency badge hangs out over a plain blue canvas jacket. Her eyes glow bright grey in the dim lighting. I don't need magic to be able to tell she's powerful.

Remy shifts, and I don't blame him based on his past experience. But she looks infinitely more friendly than the last powerful fae we encountered.

Just as fast, he relaxes. Another smile threatens my face as Agent Sara Alder steps out, looks around, and brightens significantly when she sees Remy.

Are we this bad? Athina's arm tips against mine.

Definitely not. We're perfectly logical, mature adults.

Her head tilts back in a laugh that hits my heart with a little thrill. I drag my attention from her and turn to the agents.

"Commander Volha." The fae sticks out a hand. I arch a brow as I take it.

"Sergeant O'Donnell. You're a long way from the office, Commander."

She smiles. "I like to keep my skills fresh, Sergeant. Now it looks like something just went down and your man here has a very interesting tracking spell going."

Remy scowls her direction, angling like he can shield his spell from her sight.

"Long story short, camp was attacked, traffickers made off with four kids and Doctor Novak. One of my men was able to tag along before they jumped out of here. Specialist Kalama's got the tracker going, and we're just about to head out."

"We'll send—"

"Nope." I cut her off. "You're staying here. The camp guards are all out of commission and I don't know if the traffickers will try again. We've also got some garbage for you to take care of." I nudge the fallen man with my boot. "There's a few more bodies that need to be taken care of as well."

Volha is about to protest, but I'm already waving my hand. "Let's roll."

I'm not taking any of her soldiers with me.

"Sergeant." Alder flashes a smile.

"Alder." I hold out a fist and the half-elf knocks hers against it. "Get everything organized here. We'll be back, and then you and Remy can catch up."

She turns beet red, and I chuckle as Remy glares daggers at me. Besim smirks and has to push Remy to get going. The dragonwalkers fall in with us, shaking out arms and getting ready to shift.

Once we're out of the gates and into the open space, they transform, fifty-foot dragons taking their place. Athina lowers to a crouch, giving me a step up off her foreleg. Our mental connection is always stronger when she's in dragon form. Recently I've been feeling like my vision's a little sharper, senses heightened. She's probably waiting to drop an "it's because we're mates" just to see me vomit at the word.

I settle in the space at the base of her wings between spikes. I tap the comm in my ear. "All good?"

"Yep," Besim replies.

"Tracker's still bright," Remy says.

"Rem, you and Takis take lead."

"Got it."

Takis lopes forward and launches into the air. He and Remy have done it before, and Remy will direct with a series of taps on Takis's shoulder to make sure they're headed in the right direction.

Ready? Athina's voice fills my mind.

Let's go.

17

TARA

I'm in shock.

My brain helpfully records all the signs and symptoms—elevated heart rate, increased respirations, dizziness, rising nausea—but does nothing to help me still my panicked breaths and shaking hands. I've been put in a room with the re-kidnapped kids. They're all crumpled on the floor, some starting to come to from whatever knockout or stunning spell had been used on them.

A whimpering sound pulls my attention back to myself. It's me. *I'm* the one making the noise. It gets me focusing. Clenching hands together in a fist, pushing it against my sternum, using the deep pressure to recenter myself, giving a point of contact to narrow my attention to.

It's the only thing that helped the panic attacks after the heartbond was torn away and through all the fallout after. I haven't had one in years, but after the last few hours, I'm definitely overdue for one.

My breathing regulates, and I start to settle in my own skin. The binding is gone from around my wrists, and I'm free to move. I place a hand on the dust-covered ground. There's warding all around this room, humming through the air strong enough that I don't need higher level spells to detect magic. I cautiously bring some magic to my fingertips.

Not warded against using healing magic at least. Probably against anything stronger, like someone trying to break out.

Small sobs start to fill the room, and I crawl over to the nearest kid.

"Hey, it's okay." But my shaking voice belies the comfort I'm trying to give. The girl curls away from me, covering her face and entire body shaking. Some red still circles her neck from where they'd put a binding collar on her, and we'd taken it off.

It takes another second to will some steadiness back in. "I'm Doctor Novak. You remember me?"

She pauses, and then nods, uncurling enough to give me a glimpse of a tear-filled eye through tangled black hair. A pointed ear sticks out of the mess. The tears brighten her deep green and silver eyes. Elf.

"A lot has happened, so I don't think I remember your name. Sorry. Can I check to make sure you're okay?"

The kid sits up slowly, staying curled protectively. "I'm...S-Sylvia."

"Hey, Sylvia." I smile. "You can call me Tara if you want."

"I'm...I'm not supposed to call adults by their first name." Sylvia sniffs and new tears bud along her dark lashes.

I give another smile, and this one feels closer to actually genuine. "Okay. I don't have my stethoscope or anything, so I'll be using a little bit of magic. That okay?"

She nods and lets me take her hands, placing fingers against the wrist pulse and sending a bit of magic through. Heart rate slows, and the blood pumping through her veins and arteries brings back the message that she's still got some drugging magic in her system. I refocus, working up a clearing spell, and send it in.

Sylvia relaxes, and that headache forming around her temples vanishes. I give another encouraging smile and then tell her I'm going to help her neck. She tips her chin up and I'm able to calm the redness and give a burst of accelerated healing.

I pat her hands and move on to the next kid. This is a little faster since they're all mostly awake now and saw me taking care of Sylvia. A young half-fae with a ring of bright fae purple around his brown irises, and a nine-year-old warlock with magic shushing and sighing through her veins like the ocean. The last in the line still lies on the ground, but as I get to him, he rolls over and squares off with me.

There's something a little more feral about this one. Something harsh to the lines of his young elven face. His jeans look like they'd ripped long before he'd been taken.

"I can take care of myself." His jaw sets belligerently, and as if to prove it, he clenches his fist. I get an overwhelming whiff of healing magic bursting from him. Wildly uncontrolled and raw. He's got magic, but I don't think anyone has taught him how to use it.

"Definitely looks like you can." I nod. "But maybe be careful with using so much all at once."

He scowls, and scoots back against the wall. The *you can't tell me what to do* loud and clear. It's an expression that reminds me a lot of another blond elf.

"Where's your boyfriend?" he shoots.

It halts me. Great. The *one time* I forget about Dejan is the time I might actually need him. I'd been thoroughly dazed when they'd pulled me away, and I have no idea where he is.

A thought lodges in my chest, so hard it makes my nose sting. *What if they killed him?*

It makes me retreat from the kids, finding an empty space against the wall to sit. A lot of emotions and feelings I'm too scared to process through start to rise. I've moved on, but maybe apparently not as much as I thought. Not after seeing his stupid face again and learning what that spell's doing to him.

Three of the kids bundle together, trying to find some comfort from each other in the face of uncertainty. The elf boy is still apart, sitting cross-legged, leaning against the stone like he's not worried at all.

I feel like I should apologize to them all. I'd promised they'd be safe in my camp and now they're right back where they started. Captured, no clear way out except to wherever these monsters are going to take them.

I'm not even sure why the gang took me, other than to keep the Drax Guard and dragonwalkers at bay. I might not even have a purpose anymore. So should I be counting down until I'm killed or...a shudder cuts through me. Maybe the traffickers will think they have a use for me as well.

A rattle at the door has me jumping and one of the girls screaming before she clamps a hand over her mouth. I'm halfway to them, ready to shield them somehow, when the door flies open and one of the men steps through.

He holds a steel spear, the end coated in a nasty looking spell that pops and spits red sparks. *Do not get hit with that.*

"Clear. Dump him."

He stands aside and two other men pull Dejan in. His boots drag and they've got a death grip on his upper arms. They kick his legs out from under him, and give a shove on the way down. His shoulder and head thump hard against the ground and I wince for him, but he doesn't move.

Either he's a great actor, or, more likely, he blanked out again. One kicks Dejan's low back and he doesn't respond. The man curses, and I catch something about the *bleeping* Drax Guard.

Spear guy comes over, giving the kids a once-over.

"They look fine."

And they clearly know what's on that spear, since the three are cowering more and the elf isn't moving despite his scowl and clear desire to do something.

I shrink back when the man turns to me.

"You take care of them?" he asks.

I nod before I realize I probably shouldn't respond to him.

But he just laughs, an ugly sound, and turns to his companions. "We have a spot for resident doctor, right?"

They snicker, apparently enjoying the jolting gut reaction that shows clearly on my face. The door shakes as they slam it behind them. This time my ears catch locks turning and my skin crawls a little with a sealing spell.

At least Dejan's alive and he'll know what to do. Well, maybe he's alive. He hasn't moved yet. I scoot over and tentatively poke his unfairly muscled arm. They took his vest and chain mail, and the hat is gone. Still nothing. I move a little closer.

He lies there, eyes open and staring at nothing. The binding magic is gone, but his wrists are now contained by iron-laced handcuffs. Dampening his magic if it was free.

"Dejan?" I whisper and poke again.

Nothing. Not even a blink.

My hands work open and shut a few times. A glance over my shoulder assures that all the kids are watching, but there's no cameras or anything to suggest that the traffickers are. Guess they're pretty secure in those locks and the spell.

I rest a hand on Dejan's forearm, and send out some magic. It's like I'm teetering on the edge of an abyss. There's nothing there, no trace of *him*.

I want to pull away from the emptiness, but I actually need him this time. So I pull more magic, green flickering in the corners of my vision, and search until I find a tiny path leading to a bricked-up feeling. My magic snakes through the barest hint of a crack surrounded by the same buzzing wildness of Remy's magic. But the warlock's magic is fading, losing the struggle against the stoneheart.

Closing my eyes, I squeeze tighter around Dejan's forearm, and wedge my magic into the crack. Pushing and straining until a drop of sweat trickles down my temple. He jolts as my magic snakes through, and I hit against vibrant life straining against its prison.

Something lingers in the back, calling to my magic. I can't keep it back as it races giddily over, skidding to a halt at the feel of a gaping hole, tattered edges trying to grab for my magic, desperate for something to help knit it back together.

The broken heartbond.

A tendril of my magic gets caught. Dejan surges away, coughing and gasping like he's almost drowned. I yank my hand back, trying not to press it to my chest where I definitely felt a tiny bit of something.

He yanks his wrists against the cuffs, still coughing as he pushes up to knees and awkwardly balances on bound hands. A grunt escapes and then he goes still. I worry he's lost already, but his silver-green eyes are locked on to me.

"Tara?" A hoarse edge coats his voice. I give him a little more space and he sinks back onto his heels, taking in the room, the kids, and giving me full view of a bloody face.

Then he grimaces, the shoulder he landed on pulling up. His hands press to his stomach, and he looses a string of curses that has me frowning and, "Dejan, the *kids*."

He just looks at me, then at the kids. "They don't know what that means."

"I do," pipes up the elf. He watches Dejan closely and with interest.

"Great, that one speaks Vinland slang." Dejan casts around himself and then starts to move into a sitting position.

"There's something wrong with you," the elf states.

Dejan huffs. "There's a lot wrong with me, kid."

The boy pulls his knees up, resting folded arms across them, and not turning his focus from us. Dejan slowly eases his leg out, and doesn't move his hands from over his stomach. He curses again, this time a lot more quietly.

I watch a moment, then halfway reach out. "Can I help?"

He tilts a look from the corner of his eyes. "You really want to?"

"Just let me." Frustration at him, and myself, escapes.

Dejan lowers his hands, still tensing a little as I reach out and place a hand against his stomach. Not doing more than easing the aching muscles, making sure no organs were injured. To his shoulder. This one has traces of an old injury, but right now it's just bruised and starting to swell from catching his entire weight against the ground.

A relieved breath escapes him as I take my hand away, and his posture relaxes. I want to stop working, but my healing magic buzzes in my veins, so I reluctantly reach for his face.

He freezes, but lets me pass my fingers across his skin, nudging burst blood vessels back together, and pushing the swelling and the hard-working white blood cells back towards the lymph system. They slowly move away, like they're upset at not getting to do their job.

His head's okay, other than still being thick and stupid. And I'm looking right into his eyes as I take my hand away.

"Thanks," he says softly.

I nod and sit a few feet away.

"You okay?" he asks.

He's settling me more than I want to admit. I shrug. "It's my first time being kidnapped, so not really."

"You'll be okay." He sounds certain.

I look away, over to the kids looking at us like the adults are going to know what to do. I wish I did.

"Tara, I need you to do something for me."

I focus back on him.

"I need you to get into my pants—"

I recoil, mouth dropping open.

His lips flatten and he rolls his eyes. "Pocket. My *pants pocket,* Tara."

My scowl matches his. "You could have said that."

"You jumped to the conclusion all by yourself," he retorts. "*In my pocket,* left side." He looks pointedly at it and lifts his cuffed hands, showing that he can't really do it himself.

I scoot over, still frowning, and glare at him. He just gives a flat look back.

"There's a coin." His voice is low, just between us. "Get it out and stick it in your boot or somewhere they're not going to find it."

I get beside him and he adjusts so I can slide fingers into the pocket and fish out the coin. It's warm and pulsing with a little bit of energy.

"Boot. Now." He focuses on the door. I do as he orders, and it settles against my ankle. Nothing stirs and when he finally relaxes a bit, I dare to ask.

"What is it?"

"Tracker coin. Rem and the team are on their way. Keep that and stick as close to the kids as you can. They'll get you."

A bit of hope blossoms, quashed just as fast as I parse through his words. "What about you?"

He gives a bleak smile. "My cousin never got snagged in all the arrests years ago. He's got a hit out on me now. And he's on his way to collect me. I don't know when he, or my team, is getting here, so just look after yourself and the kids."

"Dejan..."

"Just do it, Tare. I'm deadweight over here. I don't know when I'm going to blank out again, so I'm not going to be much help."

"But..."

"This way you'll finally be rid of me." His smile has no humor, and I don't know what I'm feeling again.

"Maybe I don't *completely* want to be rid of you," I say, almost against my will.

He tilts a glance at me, then looks away. "Don't go soft on me now, Novak."

I manage a scoff, but he's got a faint smile, and it pulls a small one from me. We sit in silence a moment more, before I nudge his arm.

"Thanks for coming after us. You didn't have to."

He bumps my arm back. "Wasn't going to leave you behind this time."

The quiet words bring some tears to my eyes. I'm really tired of crying or almost crying.

"Is he really your boyfriend?" the elf pipes up from across the room. All eyes are still on us.

"Nosy," Dejan states.

The kid sneers back. "What'd you give her?"

"Portal spell for everyone but nosy kids."

I roll my eyes. This part of Dejan apparently has not changed.

"You're so funny." The kid makes a face, tongue sticking out.

"I'm freaking hilarious." At least he's not cursing.

"Yeah, cops usually think they are."

One of the girls gasps and glares at the kid like he shouldn't antagonize.

"Bluejays usually aren't." Dejan seems unperturbed by the almost nonsense coming out of his mouth. Maybe I need to check further for damage.

But the kid glares. "You gonna pretend to know something, *cop*."

"Not a cop." Dejan shrugs.

"Don't be rude, Marko. Maybe he won't help us."

Marko scoffs. "He'd already have done something if he cared. Besides, he can't. There's something wrong with him."

Everyone looks at Dejan now, and he just shrugs. "Maybe there is, maybe there's not."

"I heard someone's coming for you." Marko shoots this at Dejan, like he's trying to probe for something else.

"You got good ears, Nosy." Dejan leans back against the wall, shifting like he's trying to get comfortable. He's pretending not to care, but now

I can see the coiled tenseness surrounding him. "They're going to get you in trouble someday."

Marko flicks at his right ear, and then sweeps his finger in a circle. "Already have, Bluejay."

"Then pay better attention next time."

Marko shoots off a reply that someone his age definitely shouldn't be saying, and I want to clear my throat and glare reprovingly, but there's just the hint of a smile on Dejan's face. Marko doesn't seem as surly after saying *that*, and lapses into silence, picking at the fraying edge of one of the holes in his jeans.

"Tara." Dejan's murmur is filled with an edge. Fear. I lean toward him. "I...I think I'm going to—"

He goes still. Hands settling into his lap and gaze focusing idly on nothing. I swallow hard, wishing I didn't have to see this. Didn't have to start feeling sympathy for him.

I touch his forearm again, not daring to push as hard, but finding that thread again. It's wavering, somehow now a mix of Remy's and my magic. But the stoneheart squeezes hard, agitated at the entrance of my magic and fighting back, working harder to seal itself off.

My magic shoulders its way in, maybe desperate to get to that second gaping hole, heal it, and I can barely rein it in.

Dejan inhales and is back.

18

Dejan

My chest aches, and not just from being punched a few times. Tara's hand rests on my arm and whatever she's done has made me feel enough to want to take her hand in mine. I try to move out from under her hold.

"Thanks."

She moves with me. I shouldn't be looking at her, shouldn't be searching out the depths of her green eyes, the silver spiraling around the iris. But I am, and for an instant the trapped me, able to finally get a foot wedged in the crack she and Rem helped me find, quiets.

"Dej."

Don't call me that, I want to beg.

"I think I'm making you worse."

She's right. She's been right about so many things. About me, long before she told me that I was lying to myself. The tightness in my chest is the spell winding tighter, already attacking the crack, beating *me* back inside.

But for brief minutes in time, she's making me *better.* And in the shittiest irony there is, I, who never partook of the drugs I helped sell, want to chase this feeling. Take another hit of her magic, soak in the version of me this is making.

And even if it makes me fall faster to the curse, I'd still want her to keep trying. Because it'd give me a few more minutes to try to make up for my family and everything I did to her.

"Tare."

Her features twist, a bit of misery there. She doesn't want to hear the nickname, same as I don't want to hear mine in her soft voice, but still yearn for it.

"I'm so sorry. You were right."

She shakes her head, tears forming again, and this time I do catch at her hand, squeezing tight. "Please, let me finish."

She stills, focused on our hands.

"I was always just a coward. I took the easy way out, looking out for myself. I wanted to tell you, but somewhere in there I also wanted you to have some sort of life. You're better off without me, Tare. But that doesn't mean I've stopped thinking about you and regretting everything every day for the last fifteen years."

Her face turns away, her hand tightening in mine, tensing like she's about to pull away, but she doesn't.

The year and a half after I left was spent on the streets, slowly hitch-hiking my way west to vanish onto the streets of Portland. And then I'd seen a drug overdose happen in an alley. An off-duty paramedic had stopped to help until the ambulance came. I'd watched, forced to admit I was helpless because I didn't know how to use my elven magic to heal anyone other than myself.

I'd seen the used packet with stylized lines swooping into a Shrike still clenched in the addict's hand, and I knew it would always follow me one way or another. Tara's fierce *"Don't you ever want to do more, Dej?"* echoed in my head. So I asked the paramedic how to do what he did. And a few weeks later, I'd cautiously showed up with the new cohort for class, paid for with the cash I'd taken out of Detroit. That had been the first time in almost two years thinking about Tara hadn't hurt. And on my first call, and every other one after, I thought about her and hoped she'd found some way to help people like she'd always wanted.

"And I'm really sorry that we got you pulled into this. I'm sorry it's ending this way, and I'm leaving you behind again. I'm just..." There aren't words and there aren't actions to show this, so another soft, "I'm really sorry," this time in Slavic elvish has to work.

Tara slips her hand free, rocking back, palms pressing to the sides of her head as she sniffs. "You never make anything easy, do you?"

The sight of her threatening tears drives an arrow into the crack, helping me keep it open.

"Never." The word comes with a strangled sob from Tara. "And you're just going to...*leave* again." Her smile twists, and she shakes her head. Maybe she's angry enough to move on quicker. "And what am I supposed to do?" Her shoulders lift, and she scrubs under her eyes.

I remember. I remember what to do to make her laugh. I shouldn't, but..."Maybe don't dance too hard on my grave? Definitely not to that hideous band you loved. At least give me some peace."

Tara pauses and then a faint laugh, more like a sob breaks. She shakes her head, fighting a smile and wiping her eyes again. And when she looks back to me, I'm talking again.

"My old sergeant, Pothos Allaire, is in charge of my will. Everything from the last fifteen years was always going to have gone to you if anything..." Part of me had hoped that I'd go out on a mission someday. Something quick, and not like this.

She stares at me, and I crook a smile. "Least I could do."

Tara shakes her head, probably ready to refuse it and any other link to me.

"Just take it," I say. "Start some foundation for the really cranky dementia patients. Name it after me."

A smile threatens behind the halfhearted glare she's trying.

"I know Rem and Bes have some really horrible pictures of me. Put one in the hallway."

Another wipe to her eyes. "Well, now those I have to see."

"On second thought, maybe my dying wish will be all photographic evidence burned."

But there's a vague friendliness in her gaze.

"If you two kiss, I'm going to barf."

"Marko!" one of the girls hisses. Tara and I swing our attention over to them. Marko looks absolutely disgusted. The two girls might as well have hearts pulsing in their eyes as they watch us, and the other boy is giving a fairly solid impression of trying to melt into the floor in embarrassment.

And Tara looks about the same way. At least until we look at each other and I give a wry tilt of my brow. "Could be a pretty good distraction."

She rolls her eyes, lightly swatting at my arm and scooting several inches away. Something about her putting some space between us makes the stoneheart push harder, and I'm back to struggling to keep that bit of awareness again.

Tara glances to me, lips parting, and I'm ready to hang on to the promise of her saying something, anything, when the locks clicks. One of the traffickers steps through, ensorcelled spear at the ready.

And I'm not prepared for the almost physical punch in the gut as my cousin enters the room.

19

DEJAN

DAMIR BARELY LOOKS A day older than when I left, but he still sports dark slacks and tightly fitted dress shirt and vest, all tailored to enhance his lean, muscular form. Blond hair is cropped close, diamonds in his earlobes and a slender gold chain around his neck. Sleeves rolled up, exposing a knife sheath on his tattooed forearm. He's got smaller knives hidden everywhere.

He locks on to me with a slow smile that doesn't reach his eyes. "De'janick. The prodigal son."

"Da'mirchen. The Butcher himself."

His smile thins. "Here to finally do the deed."

From the look of the rings on his right index and ring finger, he took over after Dad got three life sentences. And he's clearly done well, since he's not dead and still has the money to dress like that. Guess the bag of cash I took with me as a parting gift and *fir you* didn't set anyone back at all.

Damir glances around, not interested in the kids, but then his eye settles on Tara. The smile spreads again, lighting something darker in his eyes. For the first time, I'm glad I can't feel much of anything, because I'd be almost feral at the look he's giving her.

"Tar'amischa Novak. As I live and breathe."

She doesn't say anything, just stiffens. She never met him. No one met Damir back in the day unless Dad needed a silent threat in any business meeting, or they'd messed up. Then he'd be the last thing they saw. I guarantee her father met Damir.

He tilts a finger from me, to her, then back to me. A laugh, and he claps his hands together, folding forward slightly like he's just been told the funniest joke on earth. And it's never good when he laughs. "The *odds* of finding you two out here together. I'm surprised she didn't try to kill you first, Dejan."

I give her a small shake of my head, warning her not to engage. But Damir catches it.

"Oh, don't tell me that he softened you back up?" He tosses a hand. "Did he give you some speech, some soft 'I'm sorry'? He's always been good at spinning words." This is leveled at me. I just stare back.

Competition had always reigned in our house, but sometimes we'd banded together for a mutual cause. Before we'd started our separate paths within the Kostic clan.

"Rafe," he calls over his shoulder and a bulky dark-haired Nordic elf shoves past the guard, scorn in his eyes. So this drug dealer thinks he's above a trafficker.

"Help Dejan someplace we can talk while we wait for Nathan to be ready to gate again." He turns away, then pivots back to Linten, boots hiding blades in the toes scraping against the stone. "You don't mind if I borrow the doctor, do you?"

This time I jerk against my cuffs, wrestling my arm away from Rafe's grip for a moment. Damir smiles slowly, and Rafe pins me again.

"Come on, Dejan. You're better than that." He *tsks*. "Besides, how do you know she's not going to want to see this?"

"No. Don't!" A bit of terror fills Tara's voice as Damir snags her arm and hauls her up. She freezes at the shimmer of a knife blade in his hand.

"Walk," he says quietly.

I get one last glance at the kids. They're confused and terrified, but not as much as Marko, who's plastered to the wall, eyes fixed on the shrike tattoos on the right side of Damir's and Rafe's necks. He knows what those mean.

I never got one, playing the role of distraction for the cops and the Feds, the "favored" kid who wasn't in deep with the clan. The one who went to the fancy schools, got the good grades, and didn't get caught as the local dealer. The one who masqueraded as a college student, making deliveries. Until the day I met Tara and the deeply hidden desire to get out became a fully-fledged plan.

"Keep those ears out of trouble," I remind him before I get shoved through the door. Tara's lighter tread falls a half-beat off from Damir's near soundless boot falls.

We barely make it into the main room before Rafe lays into me. Every hit makes the traffickers' punches earlier feel like love-taps. I'm on the floor, gagging and spitting out blood, ribs cracked and lungs rattling before my delayed processing catches up.

Even then, the pain isn't fully present. It's like there's two versions of me—one lying here, vaguely aware of the blood and pain, and another which wants to give voice to the agony and rage but *can't*.

Damir's just getting started. All I can do is endure, try to protect Tara if I can, and wait for the others to get here.

20

Tara

I watch in horror as the elf strikes Dejan over and over, wishing I could shield my ears from the *sound* the impacts make. He steps away, leaving Dejan crumpled, wheezes barely making it past bloody lips. His cousin takes a pendant from Rafe and clenches it tight in his fist, speaking some word I don't understand before pressing a hand gleaming purple and silver to Dejan's stomach.

It absorbs into him, twisting and contorting his body. He's in agony but something about his eyes, the muted cry, tells me he can't feel it. Or is trapped inside himself with the pain.

"Stop." The word whispers from me and I pull against my captor.

Damir slowly stands, leaving Dejan to be hauled to his knees by Rafe. The Butcher turns to me.

"You sure you don't want to watch this?" he asks me. "After what he did to you?"

I hated Dejan for what he did. Thought I hated him. But never like this.

"You know." Damir prowls closer. "Maybe it's a good thing he ditched you. All he does is betray people. He didn't seem to think twice about cutting that heartbond out." He pauses, sweeping a glance between us.

"Never had a binding ceremony either." He leans closer. "So maybe he was never planning to be loyal to you anyway."

Dejan hunches over and spits out blood. Damir's words would sting more if we hadn't already talked, if I hadn't already seen the way he'd changed. Hadn't heard how he'd jumped to save his crewmate from the stoneheart. Hadn't watched him work with me to stitch up Athina, watching him *care* about something, maybe for the first time ever.

If he hadn't spoken the truth about us and how we saw the heartbond and each other. Because he was right. I'd wanted out too but wasn't brave enough or strong enough to tell my family what I really wanted. He felt like something forbidden, and I was projecting all my dreams on him, and was going to be disappointed when it was inevitably impossible to live up to them.

"Did no one ever tell you to be careful of Kostics?" Damir pivots and kicks Dejan in the stomach. It's the same muted cry as before. Dejan slowly lifts his head, bound hands pushing against the ground.

My heart rises in my throat as Damir comes toward me, pulling a knife.

"I'm disappointed you don't have a heartbond anymore, too." His smile is eerie, predatory. "I was specifically ordered not to touch either of you years ago. I missed my chance to see what happens in a heartbond."

Silver flashes and cold steel presses against my cheek. A whimper locks in my throat as it presses but doesn't cut. "I think your father would be happy to see you again, don't you think?"

I haven't really talked to my parents in months. It hasn't been much deeper than formalities over the last fifteen years. Learning that my father was working for the Shrikes as he got arrested broke a lot in our relationship. Dejan wasn't the only one leaving betrayal and lies in his wake.

Damir takes another pendant and activates it. My heart seizes as he reaches toward me. Searing cold presses against my forehead and pain lances through my mind. Nausea surges up in response to memories of the last day skidding all over the place, but the moments with the Drax Guard soldiers are crystal clear. Suddenly, it's still, my mind going blank for terrifying seconds before my eyes focus back on Damir.

"That was incredibly helpful," he says with a smirk.

"Leave...her...alone." Dejan's labored words only brighten Damir's smile.

"And what are you going to do about it, cousin?" he asks, gaze not moving from mine.

I try to hold it, stare back like I'm not petrified. He'll hurt me without blinking, but I think only because it'll hurt Dejan. We just have to hold out until his team gets here. But I don't know when that'll be. And I'm not sure what Damir just did to me.

"Nothing." It whispers from my dry throat. "He'll do nothing."

Damir laughs and steps away. "You hear that, Dejan?"

I have a full view of Dejan's fractured body again and my heart breaks at the bloody look he gives me.

"I'm sorry." His lips move with barely a sound. I want to tell him that it wasn't true, that I know he'd protect me. He's already tried.

But Damir pulls a knife and attacks him again and I shut my eyes against the violence.

Please, please. I beg God, the Fates, whoever is listening. This has to stop. I couldn't watch him slowly die before and I can't watch this now.

21

Dejan

Rafe hauls me up by my shirtfront, metal-covered knuckles pulled back to deliver another punch to my face, when Damir stops him.

"I want something left when we make it back to Detroit."

Rafe yanks me higher and deposits me in the tetanus chair. I list to the side, blinking as the room spins and teeters. I don't need my magic to know that I'm fractured all over from Rafe, from Damir, and from the foreign magic still slicing through me.

"There's something different about you, Dejan." Damir slides forward, head cocked to the side. "You should be fighting back. Shouldn't have gotten caught by these..." He flicks a knife around the room, taking in Linten and his scowling men with the action. "Not with the skills I know you have, plus being part of the Drax Guard."

He scoffs. "And that. Really? Playing soldier? You believe that old Kostic saying about earning back your name through righteous action?"

I lean further and spit a trail of blood on the ground. Maybe I did, maybe I didn't. He yanks my head back, pushing until I'm craned uncomfortably far against the low back, and sets his knife against the tip of my left ear.

"Maybe I'll cut them off," he muses. Cut the tips from my ears. That's an old mark of dishonor, one some groups still carry over from centuries past.

But the white noise is starting up again, low, like the distant hiss of waves on the lake shoreline. A bright sting across my cheek barely registers and it's not until Damir steps back, wiping his dagger on a handkerchief that I realize he cut me.

He moves over to Tara, tucking away the handkerchief and spinning the knife around his fingers. Her horrified look turns from me over to him, and another henchmen keeps tight hold of her arm.

"And you." He circles around her. I'm starting to fade. I can't. Not now. I move, putting pressure on my injured ribs, hoping the pain will shock me into staying present like it has before.

Barely.

"No heartbond to use against the two of you, but you'll do nicely to keep motivating your father, Miss Novak." He rocks back on his heels, glancing between us again. "Oh—" he clicks his tongue again—"Dejan might have saved you from being used in some of this, but your father is still in deep."

Guess he hadn't gotten smarter, or Damir had, more likely, found every weakness to keep pushing and now has the final piece in his hand. It's getting louder in my head, and not even Tara's pleading expression turned on me, almost begging me to do something, can shake it.

Steel presses to her cheek, pushing, coaxing a drop of red, but I'm fading, losing my footing in the crack, getting shoved back. This time getting to watch the world fade away instead of just falling into blackness.

Her lips move, and—

—and I'm on the floor, injured lungs cramping around a new hit, my cheek pressed against the stone. Tara screams my name, struggling in my periphery, but my body spasms from the pain of the impact and I *can't breathe.*

A boot comes for my stomach and my arm blocks part of it, but not enough. The buzzing grows in my ears, and I'm *trying* to stay present.

Damir grabs my shirt and slams my back into the ground. "What the hell is wrong with you?"

I can only blink before his magic-coated hand slams against my forehead, pinning me to the ground. He yanks back, staring at me, and then gives a bewildered laugh.

"You're *firred*, Dejan." He pushes to his feet, leaving me there. I can't move. Everything hurts too bad.

Damir laughs again, that same confusion rampant as he circles me. "Who did you tangle with?" He inspects his hand, rotating it like that's going to help him figure it out. "That felt fae. Also feels a little like justice."

A groan tears from my bleeding lips as I force myself to roll over, trying to push up on shaking arms. His kick to my elbow sends my face precariously close to the stone.

"This takes some of the fun out of it." He paces around me. "But I'll still take you home, figure out how to keep you conscious."

But I've only got eyes for Tara. She strains against her captor's hold, her arms pinned behind her. Then she stops, attention jolting down to her boot, then to me. The buzzing falters.

They're here.

The earth shakes, a deep guttural roar tears through the passageways. Dragonwalkers. The sharply edged scent of smoke marks Remy.

Just in time.

Another quake and then the traffickers and Damir's men spring to action. Rafe starts to drag Tara back but she's fighting. Damir yells at Linten. Weapons clash in the distance and a sharper *crack* overrides it all.

Remy's through their wards, and all hell is about to break loose.

The building shakes, dust and bits of stone starting to fall. Tara is wrenched side-to-side, her head snapping dangerously. It stuns her enough for Rafe to start pulling her toward the hallway. I can't let them take her away. I have to try to protect her this time. Damir stabs Linten and yells at someone else.

I can't hear past the roaring in my ears. They've left me on the floor and I have to get to—

22

Dejan

23

TARA

HE'S MOVING. AND THEN he's not. Something about the way his body goes limp, his head resting against the ground, that tiny piece of my magic still clinging with a death grip to the edge of his broken heartbond. And I know. He's gone. This time, he's really gone, and nothing is bringing him back.

The tracker in my boot pulses hot. It's chaos. Fighting happens somewhere, and men yell. Noises I can only assume are fully shifted dragons come from outside, maybe even stomping through the roof with how much it shakes.

But Dejan just lies there. *And I can't leave him.*

Rafe pulls on my arms, twisting them to try to get leverage to pull me back. Damir gives one look at his cousin, and then shakes his head and leaves him.

My throat aches and screams barely register in my ears. Mine.

De'janick, get up! Get up, you stupid, stupid elf.

Not like this. *Not like this.*

I stomp on Rafe's foot and his grip loosens in surprise. I pull one arm away, trying to gain momentum to keep tearing free, but more hands catch me and haul back.

"We need to get out of here," Damir snarls. "Where's Nathan?"

"Dragons, boss!" someone else shouts. "He's down."

Damir hurls a curse. "Keep bringing her. We're clearing a way out."

Rafe is too strong, and yanks me into the hallway. Another quake rips through, tossing us into the wall. An ominous groan draws my attention up, cracks forming in the ceiling.

Rafe curses and tries to hustle me along, but everything starts to collapse. I catch a glimpse of grey and blond as something heavy takes me to the ground.

24

Dejan

...

...

...

...Tara...

A sliver pierces the darkness.

And...

25

Dejan

...I'm back.

I'm back and alone in a room that's crumbling around me.

No.

Not alone.

Shouts and ominous cracking draw my attention to the far hallway. A glimpse of Tara, and I push, straining to get upright. Each ragged breath stabs through my chest and stings bleeding lips. I don't know what I'm going to do, but I'm not giving up without a fight. Halfway up, and my knee slams back down. Blood drips into the dust, the iron cuffs around my wrists hampering movement.

Again.

And then I'm limping, dragging myself forward step after step. Debris rains down. A stone strikes my shoulder and tries to throw me off course.

Onward.

Into the hallway where they're three precious steps ahead, halted by the shuddering floor and cracking ceiling. I lurch forward, slamming a shoulder into Rafe, knocking him away in his surprise. Tara cringes back. Grey light spears through, slashing across her terrified face before the broken section falls.

I yank my bound hands over her head, pushing her down, sheltering with my body as the ceiling collapses. Rocks rain down, and Rafe's cry abruptly cuts off. Nothing hits us. Tara curls under me, her arms sheltering her head. My arms brace beside her, cuffed hands pressed against her head like that was going to save her.

We should be crushed.

"Dej?"

Relief body slams me. "Rem."

I crane my head around to see him on his knees, listed to the side, arms outstretched and shaking, hands spread wide. He'd caught it. Caught the damn ceiling before it crushed us.

With a grunt and a twist of his entire body, he flings it away. I press closer to Tara at the rattle of the debris. I need to get up, make sure she's still breathing. But...delayed agony rips through me, seizing my entire body. Heightened at Remy's hands on my spasming shoulders.

He curses, but wiggles an arm under my chest, helping lift me off her. Muted sounds escape me, peppered with wheezing breaths as I try to move. He ends up doing most of the work, my limbs jerking and twitching and refusing to move correctly. I'm wishing for the part that can't feel pain to come fully back.

"Shit, Dej." Remy tilts my head upright as he settles me against the wall.

"What...what took you so long?" Oh *fir*. My left eye is swollen, compressing my vision. My right leg is completely numb. Fractured in at least one place.

"Don't move."

No problem there. My head tips forward, a streak of red dribbling down to glisten against the muddy mess of dirt and blood covering my clothes. Remy keeps one hand against my shoulder, holding me up, as he reaches for Tara.

"Doc? You with me?"

She flails, launching upright, eyes wild as she scrabbles backward, hands tearing over the stones.

"Hey, hey!" Remy keeps his hand outstretched.

I want to help, want to reach out, but my limbs aren't working. She blinks. Breathes. Then sobs. Grabs his arm. Remy gently grips her forearm and gives a calming burst of magic, based on how fast she centers.

And then she sees me. "Dejan?" Her hands take over holding me up while Remy undoes the cuffs with a sharp word.

He taps his comm. "I got him and the doc."

"Kids?" I mumble, blood trickling between my lips.

"Athina's got them," he replies.

"My...my cousin...west side." Everything spins in and out and my chest is about to implode. I catch Remy's confused face, but can't explain.

Tara does. "Drug dealer. He's getting away with some other guys." She points down the hall.

"Uh, okay. Cir, sounds like we got more than the traffickers in here. West side." He pauses. "Got it."

"Dej." Tara's hand is on my cheek, turning me gently. "You were gone."

My arm shakes and almost doesn't make it high enough for my hand to close around her forearm. "C-couldn't leave you again."

I messed up years ago. But I'd chosen her once, even if it was poorly. I have no idea if, after everything, she'd even want to give me, give us, another chance. But if she did, if I could break the stoneheart, I'd choose her again. Doesn't matter how many lives, how many chances. I'd choose her. It's only ever been her.

And the something that had cracked in my chest, *snaps*.

Fire rips through my veins, keening filling my ears. My limbs flail, head bashing back against the wall. Arms circle me and I struggle to get away, begging them to help, fighting to just keep breathing.

"I got you, Dej, I got you," Rem's voice hums in my ear. Blurred vision swings around, trying to find what hit me, why my heart is engulfed in fire.

Tara fills my narrowed scope and another *crack* ricochets. Remy keeps me from convulsing, but then something different, somehow more real, hits. A sodden feeling spreads through the left side of my chest. I choke.

New feeling ripples through me. My magic.

Broken ribs. Punctured lung.

I can't breathe.

Then her hands thrust out, connecting with my chest. My mouth works uselessly, filled with blood, trying to tell her to stop. Her eyes gleam silver, pouring unfiltered magic into me, stopping the destruction. Mine leaps to meet hers, coiling in my veins, pulling it along to each injury, knitting it faster than it should be.

Then disregarding everything else, and heading straight for my heart.

26

Tara

He's not dying.

Not here. Not broken and thrashing in his crewmate's arms.

Not until I can tell him thank you.

Remy doesn't stop me, not as I channel my brightest healing magic into Dejan. He just holds his friend as Dejan bucks and writhes in his arms.

Dejan's magic is free, cavorting and teasing mine. I don't have time to question it, focused on his ribs and punctured lung, fractured humeral head, lacerated liver...the list is too long. He's bleeding everywhere, inside and out.

My heart pounds, skin tingling at the raw amount of magic. I should stop. I need to stop. He's technically stable, but it's like I can't.

His magic has a pull on mine, and it takes over, racing towards that gaping hole, the path now unobstructed by the stoneheart. The frayed edges of the heartbond grab at our magic, reeling it in. Knitting a corner back together, then weaving across the hole. Twined magic gathers in a tidal wave and then races back along the path, tracing through me and striking straight at my heart.

I gasp, hands clenching in his bloody shirt. A touch on my wrists draws my eyes to his. And he pushes my hands away.

The awe at the heartbond trying to regrow is quashed at the realization that he stopped me. Nothing in his battered face gives him away for the two heartbeats before the magic settles, fizzing out like sea foam.

His eyes slide closed and even the knowledge that he's just unconscious, not trapped behind a spell wall, is just a fact. It's nothing before the knowledge that he doesn't want the heartbond back.

27

CIERAN

THE TRAFFICKERS PICKED THE biggest building in the Wastelands and then didn't fortify it. Remy was through their wards in seconds, and then the rest of us ran a three-pronged attack.

Remy and Athina took west, following the tracker and going for the kids and Novak. Besim and Iosef took east, and Takis and I went through the back. Systematically clearing halls and rooms, getting updates from the others as we went. Athina and Rem split when they found the kids, the four taken from camp and two others in another room. He followed the tracker to Novak.

Takis and I encountered three traffickers who tried to fight instead of surrender. We obliged. The agents had probably wanted live prisoners to question and keep getting more intel, but none of us were going to lose sleep over this.

Remy's update that there are more than traffickers has Takis jumping out of an open window to shift and fly around to give backup on the west side to Besim and Iosef. I continue on, making it to a room filled with monitors and noise coming from a hallway.

"I got you!" Remy's voice rings out. I tear across the room, skidding to a halt and taking a hammer to the heart at the sight of Dejan, barely recognizable under all the blood, thrashing in his arms before Novak hits him with healing magic.

Remy struggles to keep Dejan still, and I'm just watching, hoping, praying—I'm not really sure. Just bracing for the news that I've lost another crewmember. Another brother.

Tara sinks back, wavering unsteadily. I drop to a knee, throwing out a hand to stop her from keeling backward into the rubble. Dej lies unconscious in Remy's arms. I catch the faint rise and fall of his chest. He looks slightly more intact than he did seconds ago.

"Novak, you okay?" My boots crunch over fallen stone as I move around to look her in the face. She blinks, hands tucking up under her arms and leaning over them.

I'm not really sure if she's about to cry or pass out, but neither of those are very good options. I wave a hand at Remy. He understands and twists a little to bring his pack within better reach. I dig out another chocolate bar from the side pocket.

She reaches for the chocolate with shaking hands. I unwrap it before handing it over. Dried blood crusts her neck and cheek, but there don't seem to be matching cuts. Pupils are dilated, and she folds over again, this time some sobs escaping.

I gingerly push her back up, rubbing her shoulder, and nudging her to start eating. I really need her to be able to walk out of here on her own two feet.

"Breathe for me, Doc."

The bar crumbles as she folds her hands into fists and pushes them against her sternum. Whatever works. She comes back, slowly eating tiny bits of chocolate every few breaths. Once she feels steady enough, I look to Remy.

Dejan hasn't moved, and Remy's not giving up his hold. He checks a pulse on the side of Dej's neck and nods.

"Just unconscious, I think." *I hope*, is what he's actually saying. Because both of us are about as useful as fish out of water when it comes to healing. Though Novak seems to be coming around.

"He's s-stable," she says.

"Okay." I tap her shoulder. "How are you doing?"

She lifts her face slowly, and a tear streaks down her cheek. "I'm o-okay, I'm…"

"Deep breaths," I instruct, pushing her clasped hands back against her chest and gently keeping them there. That seemed to help before and it's helping again. "Close your eyes."

She obeys.

"Breathe in for four, three, two, one, and out for five," I count her down. Three more times before she opens her eyes and musters a faint smile.

"I don't think I'm going to throw up anymore."

"Hey, that's good." I grin, keeping her hands in place. "Rem's got a weak stomach. I don't need him hurling too."

I get a kick to my side from Remy and a tremulous smile from Novak. "One more time for me."

She focuses on my vest. Direct eye contact during a breathing technique to avoid panic attacks is pretty awkward.

She okay? Athina's question comes through.

We're getting there. How are the kids?

Scared, tired, ready to get out of here. She sends a mental image of the six kids grouped together. I appreciate the picture. It's how I tend to think, but she usually thinks in words. It's been interesting adapting to each other.

Dejan?

Stable. Looks like shit, and unconscious though.

She winces as I glance toward Dej again.

"Cir." Besim's voice breaks through comms. I release Novak who's breathing and looking more alert.

"Go ahead, Bes."

"We took out two guys on the west side right as two more came out. One got into a truck and headed north. Takis tried to pursue but got held up by some sort of spell the guy threw. He got away. Takis, Iosef, and I are all good."

"We know who these guys were?" I ask.

"Negative. And none of them are going to give us answers." Besim doesn't sound too regretful. "Hold up. We've got tattoos."

I tap fingers against the back of my other hand, waiting. Dej still isn't awake. Athina's waiting for me to be done with Besim, but I get the impression of her starting to move kids from wherever they hunkered down when the building started to collapse in places.

"I'm taking pictures, but it's some sort of bird." He grunts. "Takis says a shrike. Bird watching in your time off?" This is clearly directed at Takis and there's a faint sound through the comms before Besim chuckles.

"They've got a lot of different weapons, and—seriously, the amount of charms and attack spells hoarded on these guys." He scoffs. "This isn't some regular trafficking ring."

"Doc said something about drug dealers," Remy pipes up, wincing as he tries to move.

"See what else you can get off them, then get in here. We've got computers."

"Got it."

Remy nods past me and I pivot, finding a boot under rubble. Novak tracks my motion and then turns somewhat green again.

"Doc, Athina's going to be coming into that room in a minute with the kids. You want to head that way and make sure they're okay?"

She stands shakily, more than happy to get away from the body. Maybe also from us, the way her eyes are widening at me and the blood spattering my armor. Blood on an operating table probably feels different from fresh blood and bodies in a battle's aftermath.

"There's a-another body in there." She points to the main room.

Remy tips his head at my look. He's still good. I follow Novak and she turns away as I drag the body into the hall, noting that he'd been stabbed. It looks professional, but not Remy. Something went down in here and Dejan is going to be the best bet for answers. If...I rock back on my heels, watching him again. He's still out of it.

I move over to Novak. "Doc, you said he's stable."

She nods, rubbing her hands on her jeans. Frowning as they only get dirtier.

"What's the stoneheart doing?"

Novak crosses her arms. "It's gone."

"It's what?" Surely I didn't hear that right?

"It's gone," she repeats louder. "I don't know how or why, but it's gone."

My hands curl into the collar of my armored vest as a relieved breath explodes. I don't really care how, all I care about is it being gone.

"But Dej's okay? He's gonna wake back up?"

She nods, softening slightly. "He needs pain meds, a lot more healing magic, stitches, fluids, and sleep. But he'll wake up. Probably be back to himself."

"Thank the Fates. Rem!" I call.

"I heard." The relief is overwhelmingly clear in his voice.

Novak pauses, feet shuffling. "You guys really care about him?"

I like to think I'm decent at reading people. And she's darting glances Dejan's direction. Something passed between them in the last few hours, and the frostiness is melting. Though I don't think Athina would ever forgive me if I cut out our bond.

Damn straight I wouldn't, Athina growls.

Chill, hot stuff. Not a chance you're getting rid of me.

"Yeah," I say to Novak. "I haven't known him as long as the others, but he's our idiot elf."

A faint smile cracks her face, and she tilts one more look over her shoulder before joining Athina and the kids as they enter. Athina says something quietly to Tara, and then pulls her into a hug. Novak returns it almost desperately, taking a few moments to pull away and square up her shoulders.

"He okay?" Besim's deep voice has me swinging around. The half-troll kneels by Remy, one hand on Dejan's shoulder, the elf still not moving. Besim's eyes close and mouth moves soundlessly as Remy gives him the news about the stoneheart. Then he's up and crossing over to the computers, pulling out a flash drive from his vest and cuing up the screens.

I move over, hands still in my vest collar. Besim mutters something about the worst encryption he's ever seen. I watch, scanning some of the data and logs as he combs through, transferring it all over on the drive.

"We've got one alive. Iosef has him trussed. Didn't want to bring him around the kids." Besim finishes up, typing more on the keyboard.

"That and the flash drive should make the agents happy." And maybe not as pissed that we just left them.

"Get you out of some groveling?" Besim smirks.

I scoff. "That fae commander's gonna die of old age before I do that."

Besim chuckles again, still searching the screens. "Here's something else that'll make them happy." He points to something.

"Bes, I speak three and a half languages, and computer isn't one of them."

"What's the half?"

"Learning dragonwalker."

"You're disgustingly dedicated."

I whack my elbow against his arm. "Translate."

His finger runs under a string of numbers and letters. "This routes to a folder, and..." He does something and a list pops up that I can read. "Safe houses, contacts, and buyer lists. These look like locations across the eastern states. Should be enough to hit and take out the whole ring."

"Hell, yes." I slap his shoulder. "Get whatever else you can, then we're headed out."

"What are we doing with bodies and the equipment?"

"I'd say torch it, but that might spook anyone else from their organization coming through." I rub my chin. "Think we can stage it to look like these two groups went at it?"

Besim shrugs. "Should be able to."

"Let's get on that, and then head out."

One look at the kids and Novak, and I shake my head. There's another truck we could take, but we're a hundred miles into the Wastelands and driving out is going to be tricky. We're at the southern edge, but there's still plenty of creatures and latent magic ready to make a grab for us. And I'm not really interested in making another trek through it.

The three dragonwalkers aren't going to be able to carry us all and I'm loath to split the group up. Which means gating. Remy indicated on the way in that there's enough wards still active around here that should protect us from anything scampering over when he uses his magic.

I head over to Remy. "Think you can get us back?"

He sighs, cracking his neck. "I'm just requesting the next twenty-four hours off, Sarge."

My fist thumps his shoulder. "Same here."

Dejan hasn't moved. It looks disconcertingly like the stoneheart is still in place, but I'm trusting Novak. It takes time to get the bodies situated. Athina and Novak take the kids outside while the rest of us work.

"What about that monster?" Takis asks. They're deferring to me as the commanding officer with Dimos still out. Iosef surprised it outside, killing it with a dragon bite to the base of the neck. And after what it did to Dimos and Athina?

"That thing can burn for all I care," I reply. He flashes a smile that shows teeth slightly too pointed for a human-looking face and jogs off down a hall that will take him outside.

Besim gets Dejan slung over his shoulders, and I give Remy a hand up. The warlock blows a sigh and shakes his arms as we head outside.

He flicks his hands and gets ready. "I hate doing these."

I slap his shoulder. "Take your time."

He does, and is a lot steadier without battle raging all around. One of the kids, an elf, watches us from a few safe feet away.

"Bluejay okay?" he asks me finally, jerking a chin at Dejan.

I half-smile. "We're not cops. But yeah, he's okay."

He shrugs like he really doesn't care. "Thought the Shrikes were gonna kill him for sure."

"What?" Besim tilts his head. The elf backs away slightly, lips clamping shut.

"Shrikes? Those guys with the tacky tattoo?" I gesture at my neck.

A faint smirk shadows his face before he nods. "Yeah, they wanted him." He edges farther back, closing off again. He doesn't look like the other kids. They were probably snatched on their way home from school or somewhere equally innocent. He looks like he was taken from an alley and isn't going to have anyone looking for him.

Small too, smaller than an elf teen should be even with their shorter stature. I've got a feeling he's older than he looks.

"You think we could talk a little when we get back to camp?" I ask. I'm not sure who the Shrikes are yet, but them wanting Dejan specifically doesn't sound like anything good.

He sneers. "Like I'd talk to a Jay."

I shrug. "Up to you. I'll be around."

Another scoff, like I'm an idiot. But I knew a couple of kids like him growing up in foster care. He's not going to make a run for it until we're back in the city and he can take off with the supplies he'll squirrel away from the camp kitchens. I've got some time.

Remy opens up the portal, and we're through. This time right in front of the surgical building. He's last and I catch him as he stumbles.

Commander Volha stands with arms crossed, arching a brow that's probably meant to be intimidating. Agent Alder sneaks around her, helping shepherd the kids inside and casting a really long look at Remy over her shoulder.

Honestly, these two are getting ridiculous.

"If you'll excuse me, Commander, my guy's about to pass out and he's heavy."

Remy curses me under his breath, shoving some of his staggering weight into me. The commander just keeps that brow up, and then moves aside. "We'll talk later, Sergeant."

"Yes, ma'am."

The elf kid smirks a little at me and I wink back before I get Remy inside.

28

TARA

I TAKE MORE THAN my allotted ten minutes in the shower. Over half of it is spent staring at the wall, letting hot water crash over me. The Drax Guard and the dragonwalkers had shepherded me along, barely free of my daze. I'd followed them all into the surgical building, made sure that Raquel and Andrew, my elf resident, had everything under control.

I couldn't quite watch Besim unload Dejan onto a table and Andrew start triaging the still-substantial injuries. Angie led a few other nurses in checking over the team. Raquel was the one to find me standing in almost shock at the door. She hugged me, then convinced me to go shower and sleep after a cursory check over.

But when I step out and dress in long athletic pants and a clean shirt, my bed and the quiet of my room are the last things I want. An itch has started up alongside the half-repaired heartbond. It's trying to keep growing, and the feeling is like any healing scab. Except this one is not as easily soothed.

Maybe *seeing* Dejan, just checking on everyone, will help settle it a little. Just...maybe not if he's awake. I leave my boots and pull on plain sneakers, grabbing a pain pill for my aching joints, and a sweatshirt like it's going to be something I can sink into and hide in on my way out.

I'm finally aware enough to catch the new trucks parked in the compound, and see a few unfamiliar soldiers. They've got A.S.A. patches over a Bureau logo on their sleeves. I have no idea where the agents are, but if I can avoid talking to everyone for at least a few more minutes that would be great.

I slip into the surgical building. It's quiet. The two male dragonwalkers are on beds near their captain. And the Drax soldiers? I tiptoe closer.

Dejan's been moved from the surgical table to a cot. He lies on his side, IV hooked up and a portable heart monitor silently showing a normalized EKG. There's enough of the bond to know that he's still unconscious. Also enough of the bond to start trying to draw me over, finish the healing process. I lean forward, shifting weight into a step, when the memory of his gentle touch removing my hands comes back. The half-grown heartbond isn't the only thing stinging at that.

Remy is in the chair positioned at the head of the bed, leaning back against the wall, arms crossed over his chest, asleep. Cieran sits on the next cot over, the one tucked into the corner. He's up against the wall, legs sprawling over the bed's edge. Athina nestles against him, back to his side, head against his shoulder. His arm is around her and one of her hands covers his. They're both asleep, armor off, but weapons close at hand. Besim pulled up a chair to slouch in, one boot up on Dejan's cot, also asleep from his steady breathing. His weapon leans against the cot within reach.

He's our idiot elf. The sergeant's words come back. It's probably the adrenaline and fear of being kidnapped and seeing something familiar in him that had made me soften more. But maybe a little was his apology and words. Things that made me want to see how much more he'd changed. Especially now with the stoneheart gone. The way they all care about him, the way he clearly cares about them. Something I'd never seen him direct at anyone outside of me.

Leaving had been good for him. Maybe him leaving had been good for *me*. The fallout after he'd left…it'd given me the courage to ditch those finance classes I didn't understand and was only taking because Dad wanted me to. The three days in the hospital had reawoken the childhood dream of being a doctor. Seeing how fragile our family really was after Dad was indicted in the trials and had a few years' prison time…

I left after getting my degree and haven't really looked back. I wouldn't be who I am today if Dejan hadn't left. I'm still pissed that he tore out the heartbond, but…maybe I want to see if we could at least talk through everything, just the two of us.

My hand rubs my sternum, like it can soothe the heartbond still trying to get over to him and finish the repair. Though maybe he won't want to even talk since that would put us in danger of accidentally touching or looking at each other to finish repairing. And he obviously doesn't want it.

I back away, sinking down on a bench across the room. I'm a lot weaker than I thought, because this is as much of a compromise as I can get through my tired head. "Across the room" away from him, but apparently not "across camp" away from him.

"Hi." A low voice draws my look up. A woman I don't recognize stands there. "I'm Agent Sara Alder."

"Hi," I say sort of dumbly.

"Are you Doctor Novak?"

I nod and manage to extend a hand for her to shake. "Tara, please."

Sara takes a seat beside me. "I just wanted to make sure you're doing okay."

"What?" I'd been expecting eight thousand questions.

She tips a small smile. "We pieced together a little from the kids and then from Cieran's report before he passed out over there."

Cieran. She's familiar with his name.

"You know them?" I look back over to the soldiers clustered around Dejan.

"Yeah. Met them all a few months ago when I managed to get myself completely in over my head on a mission. Then got a promotion from analyst to field agent to keep working this trafficking case and sort of liaison with them." But her gaze seems to be tracking towards Remy now.

"Oh."

She flashes another smile. "After getting myself sort of willingly kidnapped by a fae, I know how insane it is to be around these guys on a mission. Plus everything else you went through, figured I'd just see if you're doing okay."

It nudges something loose inside me. "Yeah, I'm..." About to tell a lie, and my body's not going to let me. "Not really." A faint sob accompanies it.

I've never really let strangers hug me, but between Athina grabbing me in a hug a few hours ago and now this agent draping an arm around my shoulders, this might be my new trauma response. But I lean into the half-embrace.

"You don't have to be okay," she says gently. "You've been through a lot."

Tears snake down my face. "I don't normally cry in front of strangers." A hitch sneaks between words. "Or at all."

She chuckles. "I'm not judging." The gentle rub of her hand against my upper arm lets a few more tears break free.

I draw in a breath, remembering Cieran's gentle coaxing through my panic attack earlier. I use the same counting method in and out, and then I sit up a little taller. Sara pulls her arm away.

"Thanks." I manage a slight smile as I dry my face with the sweatshirt sleeve.

"You got it." She returns the expression. "Is it better for you to sleep in here rather than being off in some other room?"

I glance around, eyes always going back to Dejan. "Maybe? I just..."

"Don't want to be alone?" she finishes. "I get it."

It gets me up and moving, over to a nearby cot. She tracks down an extra blanket at my directions and brings it and a water bottle over.

One more look over before I lie down. Athina jerks in her sleep. Cieran tilts his head toward her, his other arm circling around and pulling her closer. They're both still asleep, breathing slowing again as whatever bothered her is gone in that small action.

"They're so cute," Sara mutters under her breath, smiling a little before she turns to me. "Just get some sleep. There will be plenty of time for me to pester you with questions later."

I manage to smile. "Okay. Thanks again."

She points to the bed with a mock frown. I lie down, curling up under the blanket as she leaves. I feel safer here around sleeping, but still heavily armed, soldiers. And with that realization, latent exhaustion catches up and sucks me into sleep.

29

Dejan

Awareness filters in. I think I prefer being unconscious. But my body is not letting me sink back into sleep. Magic is vibrant and pulsing in my veins, finding its way back to the nooks it waits in until I need it. Some sneaks out, wrapping muscles and veins, trying to remember the small healing spells I usually set in for missions. If the medic goes down, everyone else is screwed.

But I haven't been able to cast them in three months, so it's just sort of aimlessly wandering. Maybe that's what finally woke me. My own magic, impatient and ready to be used again.

I crack an eye open. Daylight spears in from somewhere. I'm not sure where I am, other than a cot. My eye closes, and I focus in on the room. Ears pick up breathing from several different sources. All around me, and all asleep, except...I almost smile. Besim's awake.

Fates, and they all stink. The singed Wastelands odor overlies the antiseptic smell of the surgical building. I'm not sure how long I've been here, but I'm willing to bet they've stayed the whole time. From the way they've been running for the last twenty-four hours, sleep probably was a bigger need than showers.

Something taps my foot. "You gonna say hi or just judge over there?"

I open my eyes, twitching down the blankets covering me to see Besim at the foot of the bed. His leg is propped up on the cot, arms crossed over his chest, and a tired smile on his face.

"You could have showered first," I say.

"You could have not almost died," he replies.

A smile, a real one, spears across my face. And it feels *so damn good* to have the emotion spread through me along with the expression that the smile widens a little more.

Besim drops his foot to the ground and leans on his knees. "How you doing?"

I try to move and discover...yeah, still mostly pummeled. "Been better."

He grunts. "You won't be winning any beauty pageants anytime soon."

Now that I'm talking, I can definitely feel the tightness of swelling and bruises. The heat of someone else's magic works along fractured bones all over my body, repairing the damage done by Damir and Rafe.

"Way to kick an elf while he's down," Cieran interrupts, voice still heavy with sleep.

I find him on the cot across from me, Athina sleeping against him. The tenseness is mostly gone from around his eyes, and his shoulders slope down in the same relief that fills his grin.

I can't help it. "Hey, Sergeant."

He glares back and a faint chuckle brings my hands to my ribs. My magic leaps so fast to help ease the stabbing pain that it ends up making it worse for a few seconds.

"You got a picture of him all tucked in, right, Bes?" Remy's voice is smothered by a yawn. He's at the head of the bed in another chair, rubbing his neck where it must have been tilted back against the wall.

Besim chuckles and I get a middle finger out in time for the click of the phone camera. "He's back."

It's filled with the same relief in all their faces, shining brightest in Remy's as I manage to reach my hand out for him to grip.

Fates, I don't deserve this crew. Don't deserve my old sergeant who's still checking in on me. Brothers who didn't give up on me, family I never thought I'd have. And I know they won't turn their backs on me. Not even after they hear my whole story.

"I think we're even now," I say. Remy's grip tightens around mine, but his head tilts.

"Technically, I think I'm one up on you." His other hand comes up, fingers counting. "Saved you initially from the spell, stopped you getting crushed by a ceiling."

"The ceiling was probably your fault," I grumble.

"Got us all back here in one piece."

I send a zing of magic and he just smirks as he jerks his hand away.

"Thanks," I say.

He nods, gently tapping my shoulder with a fist before standing and popping his shoulder that sometimes bothers him after it got dislocated again on a mission two years ago.

"I'm getting caffeine. Who wants some?"

Cieran raises his hand. Athina uncoils and stretches arms up overhead.

"Remy, you are an outstanding soldier and warlock, the best this crew has to offer," she says.

"Yeah, okay, I'll bring you some." Remy smiles and backs away. "Say more nice things, though."

I shake my head a little as he looks to me. What I really need is some pain meds, and to get off my own shoulder that's mostly asleep. "Bes?"

He gives me a hand to get off my side and come slightly upright, blinking at the dizziness that passes as soon as I get my magic sorted out.

Cieran tosses the pillow from his cot, and Besim uses it and mine to prop me up higher. Being horizontal had fooled me into thinking I was okay, but changing positions is alerting me to just how badly I've been injured. Between Tara's magic and whatever was used on me when we got back, they must have maxed out the amount my body would tolerate. There's always a limit to how much outside magic can be used to heal before a body starts rejecting it and turning on itself instead.

There's no ICU out here, which is where I probably should be. I'm going to have to take it slow so I don't make myself worse. Maybe even listen to a doctor for once.

A nurse comes over, checking vitals and using some low-level magic to assist. She doesn't say much. I remember her as Tara's assistant from before. The memories of the last day are a mix of blurred motion, gaps of darkness, and crystal-clear images.

Tara is nowhere to be seen, and maybe that's for the best. My heart beats strongly in my chest again and there's a faint pulse beside it. I'd felt it in the ruined hallway while she poured her magic in. Somehow it had started to regrow the heartbond, and that repaired bit is trying its damnedest to find her on the other end.

I wait until Raquel leaves to ask, "How's Tara?"

"Seems a bit shaken." Cieran rubs his right knee at the joint where skin gives way to metal prosthetic. "Dej, what's going on with you and her?"

Besim just tilts his head. He's also picking up my slight hesitation. It's really not fair to have two of them.

"I, uh...I think when she tried to stabilize me, it started to regrow the heartbond." I don't think, I know, because just mentioning it out loud has the bond pulsing brighter. It's weird to have it back, and I don't think I realized how much I missed it.

"How do you feel about it?" And now comes the psychoanalyzing. But I'm not one hundred percent myself yet, because I don't snap.

"I'm not sure."

Athina scoots to the edge of the cot and stands. "Just make sure you actually talk to her. Heartbonds aren't something you can outrun." This is accompanied by a fond look back to Cieran. "I am going to check on Dimos."

There's not much more to say. It's something I've got to figure out for myself. So I ask for the mission update instead. To which Cieran starts asking me questions that have my already aching head pounding a little more.

We piece together a picture of it all. My cousin and his Shrikes, the traffickers. One big mess. Besim shows me the pictures he took. From the descriptions they give, it sounds like Damir made it out alive. And he'll get out of the Wastelands alive too. Make it back to Detroit and start planning to come right for me.

I want Remy around for the full De'janick Kostic backstory which I'll give them before it comes out in a briefing. But he is taking *forever* with that coffee.

The reason why emerges with him a few minutes later. Sara has two mugs, and he has another two as they cross back over to us, talking and laughing about something. Besim rolls his eyes, masking the expression as they make it over and hand out coffee.

"Sergeant, whenever you're ready, we'll need to debrief," Alder says.

Cieran huffs a sigh. "Let me have about two more of these, Agent, and then we'll be good to go."

She laughs. "I'll make sure they put the decaf on."

He grimaces. "Don't do me like that, Alder. I thought we were friends."

"We are until you're wired on multiple cups of coffee in a meeting that needs a modicum of seriousness."

Remy smirks into his cup which has a tea bag hanging over the side.

"You think you know someone." Cieran shakes his head.

She only laughs. "I'm going to give this to Athina. Corporal." She gives me a nod. Somewhere in the last few months she thankfully stopped being nervous around me.

"Agent," I return.

One more ridiculous smile at Remy and then she's gone. Besim coughs lightly into his drink and Remy kicks his foot. "Shut up."

I shake my head. "It was my dying wish, Rem."

He glares at me. "And you're still alive over there."

I push some more magic into my throbbing ribs, and shift against the pillows. "There's some things you need to know before that meeting."

Cieran leans forward, and Rem sits next to him. They get the short version, but it still takes over an hour to tell it all. And the water bottle Besim gets me halfway through doesn't really help cut the tightness in my throat.

This was all supposed to have gone with me to an early grave. Not move past the vague details I'd given up about my past. Figured I could seal most of it up like my personnel records. Even in the Army, I hadn't been close to anyone. Definitely not when working as a paramedic. I was barely keeping my head above the oceans of regret, and becoming a medic was the only thing keeping me from drowning.

And then I fell in love with it. With being able to use my magic and skill to *help* people instead of just hanging back and watching them get hurt by my action or inaction. It, and serving in the Guard, feels like some sort of redemption for the years of working for my father. Maybe I do believe that saying.

"Okay, I can pull us off the mission," Cieran says. "You've got a personal connection there, and it might get complicated."

I shake my head. "The only personal connection I have is wanting my cousin to join my dad behind bars, or maybe even in the ground." I'd lost any familial love for them a long time ago. "Besides, once this is all released, Feds aren't letting me sit this one out."

Willing to bet some agents on the original case would be willing to try to pin a bunch of stuff on me. They'd been pissed that I'd gotten immunity out of my deal, and probably would *love* to see me walk in with a Drax Guard pin, an A.S.A. patch, and two commendations.

"Yeah." Cieran sighs. "Okay, well, still got your back whatever shakes out."

I don't have much energy for anything more than a nod. He's on his feet and at my side in the time it takes me to tiredly blink.

"Get some more rest, Dej. We'll be around."

Rem helps me lie back down, giving that same wordless promise. I'm asleep in seconds.

30

Dejan

I'm woken later by the nurse checking the small monitor. The others are gone, and the light has shifted to late afternoon. With Raquel's help, I get upright on the side of the bed for a few minutes. She wordlessly checks my pulse, and wraps a cuff around my wrist, the readouts giving levels of residual healing magic, my magic, and showing a steady oxygen reading from my repaired lung.

I don't need Raquel's glance over my shoulder to know that *she's* there. The nurse takes the cuff off and gives me a warning look before leaving.

"Don't turn around." Tara's low voice stops me from even working up the nerve to look her in the eye. Right. The heartbond usually activates by direct eye contact. No idea what half-repaired bonds do, but better not to risk it.

"You're doing better," she states.

"Thanks to you." I can't get my voice past this quiet between us.

The cot dips and a glance from the corner of my eye shows her sitting next to me, focus on the hands folded in her lap.

"I wanted to say thank you for coming after me. After us," she says.

A "you're welcome" sticks in my throat. I'd do it again in a heartbeat, so I just tip a nod even though she's not really looking.

"You okay?" I ask after a moment of almost painful silence. I don't need a heartbond to know the answer.

"You stopped me," she blurts. "Why'd you stop me?"

Stopped her from keeping the healing magic going, finishing the repairs.

"It was regrowing," I say.

"And you don't want it."

The accusation in her voice stops me. "No, I...I thought *you* wouldn't want it back."

A frustrated sound breaks from her, and a twinge hits my chest. "Deciding for me again?"

"Tare," I sigh, half-expecting her to storm off even though I've seen that she keeps her temper in check now. She'll pause to listen instead of launching ahead. I'm not sure how to feel that she might actually want the bond again. That she might want *me*. "I just...you'd still be better off without me, and I...I didn't want you to feel it if...if I died."

"Feel what?" she asks quietly.

"Feel the bond die again."

"You were stable."

"Barely."

She moves, an angry feeling pricking at my chest coupled with a faint sound from her.

"*Do* you want it back?" I ask cautiously.

"Does it matter? It seems like you don't."

I'm torn between laughing in shock and getting angry myself. All it took was seeing her again to make me realize how much I've missed her, how much I regret everything, and this tiny piece of the bond back to desperately want it all back. But...

"You deserve a lot better than me. Better not to have a heartbond messing that all up."

"I don't get to make that decision?" she challenges again. I almost look at her, let her see the exasperation and the longing building back up.

"Tara..."

"No, Dejan. Listen for a minute." She gathers a breath, maybe bracing for me to argue, but I wait. "Maybe I don't want someone else."

The heartbond heats and I swear it gets a little stronger.

"Maybe...maybe it might have been a good thing you left. It gave me the chance to grow up, decide what I really want. And I think it gave you the chance to do the same. You've changed, Dej, and in really good ways."

I'm not sure what to do, what to say.

"Drug dealer to Drax Guard medic." Suddenly she's close enough to nudge my shoulder with hers. "I'd like to hear how you got here, if you want to tell me sometime."

I do, and I want to know what got her here. From finance classes to doctor with her own non-profit outreach mission. "So?"

She chuckles. "Yes, I'd like to get to know you again, with or without the heartbond."

"What if it's still a mistake?" What if I'm still not good for her and break her heart again?

"The Fates don't make mistakes. That's what I'm going to believe. Surely there's a reason we met again out here, right now. You know that's probably how the stoneheart broke."

I've been trying not to think about it. "What, some act of true love? Gross." I manage to keep my voice light.

She half-laughs again and her elbow gently finds my ribs.

"Ouch," I retort.

"Sorry." But from her voice, she still smiles. Then she turns to face me. I keep my eyes locked on to the hand she holds out.

"So how about it, Dejan? Take a chance?"

A smile tugs the corner of my mouth. I take her hand and slowly lift my eyes to hers. "Always."

As I look into her green and silver eyes, a gentle thump hits my chest. Maybe it's because the heartbond is halfway there already. Maybe it's because I've felt it activate before, but it's calmer and steadier this time.

Until she smiles and then the piece of me that's been missing for the last fifteen years locks into place. Like when the stoneheart broke, this feels almost audible. Tara's eyes glisten and I can sense her same aching relief to have each other again.

We're both far from perfect, but this time, we know how to help each other when we eventually stumble. And this time, I'm never giving her up.

I lean forward, gently resting my forehead against hers. "Thanks for bringing me back," I whisper.

She gently brushes the edge of my jaw before resting her hand over my heart as she replies, "Always."

There's a lot to figure out, a lot to talk about, but for now, it's just her and me and the heartbond growing stronger, soothing the last ragged bits of my heart.

The End

The Series Concludes...

Shrike

Half-fae Maya Lyons left Detroit and her brother and his criminal ties behind over a year ago. She's settled in Dunhare to finally work on that architecture degree she's always wanted, and where the most dangerous thing is a friendship that's maybe growing to something more with Specialist Besim Antilles. Until her brother re-appears along with his boss, the most notorious elf drug lord in the Allied States. They know she has ties to Crew Six, and they want vengeance.

Communications Specialist Besim Antilles isn't sure what's between him and Maya, but when she calls him to warn the team, he and Crew Six face off with an enemy once more. It will take every bit of his skill and faith, but Besim is determined to keep both her and his team safe.

Corporal Dejan Kostic had hoped to never see his cousin again. But the past always has ways of catching up. His team didn't abandon him when they learned the hard way about his ties to a notorious crime family, and he's going to repay that trust however he can. Even if he's now got more to lose than just his crew.

The streets of Dunhare turn into a chessboard—Crew Six against the Shrikes. But not all allies can be trusted. And not everyone will emerge unscathed.

Coming 6.11.25

Preorder Now!

Acknowledgements

I didn't expect so many people to love this grumpy elf medic so much. And it might come as no surprise that he gave me trouble for this book. Not because he wasn't ready to do whatever it took to save Tara and his team, but because he would *not* open up about his past until midway through the first draft. Which, as you might imagine, changed things significantly.

But with every piece I finally pried free, nothing surprised me. And it gave me new appreciation for the elf who was coming more and more vibrantly to life with every word written in this series.

I wrote these first four books well out of order from what they're published in. And spent months working on characterization and edits to streamline worldbuilding and backstories and personalities among all four books. To see it all come together in this final version has been incredible for me, and I hope you find it just as special.

And I'm so thankful that you survived the cliffhanger of Conduit, and made it through this one to the end. If you're a Dejan fan, I hope you love him more now. And I hope you keep loving the team. We've got one more adventure to go with them and, as I always promise, it's going to be one heck of a ride.

Thanks again and always to Jenni and Brigitte for being my beta readers and for yelling at me for this one. To Gillian who squeezed in a last-minute read to give me some more feedback that put the finishing shine on this book. To Deborah for the copyediting and fangirling. And for yelling at me too. Yes, I know what I did.

To family and friends for supporting me in my author career. To the readers who have come along and fallen in love with Crew Six and this world. I can't do it without you.

And thanks to our Creator and Story-giver. I can't do it without Him either.

More Books by C.M. Banschbach

The Drifter Duology

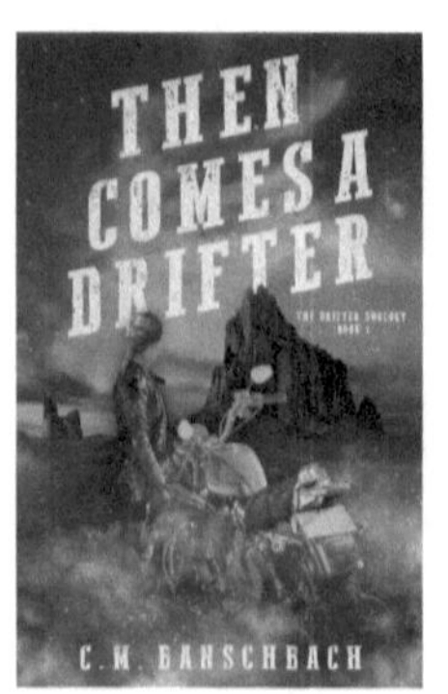

Laramie was born to ride the desert wilds. And she won't let anything stop her, even a fearsome warlord who wants her captive–or dead.

A genius mechanic–and a rare descendant of the once-magical Itan–Laramie drifts from dusty town to dusty town in search of the family that was taken from her.

But her rambling desert journey becomes a game of survival when Laramie crosses a ruthless warlord's territory. Taken prisoner by one of the warlord's biker gangs, she befriends a quiet, dangerous man named Gered. After surviving hellish circumstances Gered is tired of fighting for a better life.

Laramie will always fight. And she'll stop at nothing to win their freedom.

Enjoy this pulse-pounding motorcycle adventure in a post-apocalyptic western setting with found family and being brave in brutal circumstances. Complete series available!

The Spirits' Valley Duology

A man born for war. A bastard raised in contempt. Only together can they defend their tribe from slaughter.

Fierce-hearted Comran is the chief's son and the favored choice to be the next leader. Then his father chooses Comran's half-brother Etran for the role, straining the loyalties of the tribe and reinforcing the distance between the two men. When Comran is offered the role of battlewolf, he is ready to do his duty—but expects no friendship in return.

Steady Etran has long been shunned as the chief's bastard. Becoming the chief brings even more hostility, so he offers Comran the title of battlewolf to maintain tribal unity. But can he trust this reckless warrior as his general when Comran has never stood by his side?

As tensions mount within the tribe, a traitorous act leads to war. Comran and Etran must overcome their inner demons and fight for their brotherhood before the Greywolves fall to their worst enemies.

Read now!

———

Subscribe to C.M. Banschbach's newsletter for free short stories and book/publishing updates! http://eepurl.com/gwcGjD

About C.M. Banschbach

C.M. Banschbach is a native Texan and would make an excellent hobbit if she wasn't so tall. She's an overall dork, pizza addict, and fangirl. When not writing fantasy stories packed full of adventure and snark, she works as a pediatric Physical Therapist where she happily embraces the fact that she never actually has to grow up.

She writes clean YA/MG fantasy-adventure as Claire M. Banschbach.

Facebook – https://www.facebook.com/cmbanschbach

Instagram – https://www.instagram.com/cmbanschbach/

Website – https://clairembanschbach.com/

www.ingramcontent.com/pod-product-compliance
Lightning Source LLC
Chambersburg PA
CBHW020037310726
48970CB00007B/2298